Little Miss Evil

Bryce Leung
&
Kristy Shen

SPENCER HILL
MIDDLE GRADE

Spencer Hill Press Middle Grade:
An imprint of Spencer Hill Press, LLC

Contact: Spencer Hill Press, PO Box 247, Contoocook, NH 03229, USA

Please visit our website at www.spencerhillmiddlegrade.com

Leung, Bryce, 1982
Shen, Kristy, 1982
Little Miss Evil: a novel / by Bryce Leung and Kristy Shen - 1st ed.
p. cm.

ISBN: 978-1939392091 paperback
ISBN: 978-1-939392-10-7 e-book

Summary: A thirteen-year old girl must stop a nuclear bomb her super
villain dad created from destroying the world while keeping herself
from being captured by his super villain enemies.

The author acknowledges the copyrighted or trademarked status and
trademark owners of the following wordmarks mentioned in this
fiction: Darth Vader, iPod, John Lennon, Star Wars, Wikipedia, World
Series, Zippo

Cover design by Lisa Amowitz
Interior layout by Jennifer Carson

Printed in the United States of America

To our ridiculously short attention spans, without whom we would've never been able to publish a— **OOH, A KITTY!**

WITHDRAW

Don't let the adorable cover fool you, Little Miss Evil is one wild, adrenaline ride of absolute action packed excitement and I adored every single minute of it! It was hysterically funny and intensely suspenseful and just a crazy fun read. I mean how often do we get to root for the bad guys? Clearly not enough because Fiona and her evil father are two of my favorite characters and I'm going to be banging on Spencer Hill's door for the sequel. Hurry up guys! I need Little Miss Evil 2 NOW!

-Ellen Oh, founder of We Need Diverse Books and author of the Prophecy series

When your dad's a cackling super-villain, you get some pretty weird stuff for your birthday. When I turned six, he gave me a samurai sword. On my tenth birthday, he gave me a Universal Remote Detonator. Point it at any electronic device and it blows the device to smithereens. Last year, he gave me a laser torch disguised as a tube of lipstick. Only I didn't know that, and I almost melted my face off when I tried to put it on. So today, on my thirteenth birthday, I really don't know what to expect.

"Open it, Fiona!" Dad beams, handing me a huge box, white with a red ribbon, and then stroking his goatee. He does that whenever he's pleased with himself. Somehow, that makes me even more nervous.

Hesitantly, I pull off the lid, and inside there's a golden rectangular object small enough to fit in my pocket. A lighter?

I breathe a sigh of relief. No live grenade, no mutated anthrax. Just a normal, non-insane gift. I didn't think he was capable of that. "Thanks, Dad." I grin. "I love it."

"No, no, no. That's not your gift. That's just part one." I bite my lip, while his grin is so wide it fills up his face.

"What do you mean?"

"Oh, I could just tell you. But why tell—when I can show!" He pauses, puffing up his chest, before announcing, "To the weapons laboratory!"

As I watch him scamper off, cackling like a hyena, I can only think, no good can possibly come of this.

"Are you sure this is safe?" I ask.

"Oh, yes. Definitely! I designed it specifically for you."

Black metal covers my arm from fingertips to elbow, like a bionic limb. It's slightly heavy—as if a cast has been wrapped around my wrist—and while I can lift it, it takes some effort. Clear rods run up and down each side, and something liquid flows through them.

Dad looks so happy he practically glows. "Light it!"

"Light it?" I gawk at him and then down at the gold lighter in my other hand. "Are you sure?"

"Of course I'm sure. Put the flame right there." Dad gestures to a pinhole right below my wrist.

Okay, relax. He's most likely tested this thing. It probably won't blow up, taking my arm along with it. I'll be fine. Right?

I open the lighter and flick the yellow flame to life. Cautiously, I hold it under my wrist until the flame licks it like an impatient puppy.

WOOMF!

My arm lights up. Yellow, orange, and blue flames race through the glass rods. Somehow the rods contain the flames, and I barely feel any warmth.

I open my fingers and notice a tiny nozzle embedded in the metal on my palm. My heartbeat quickens.

Oh God.

This contraption is a flamethrower, isn't it?

"Dad, I don't think this is a good—"

"Oh, stop it," Dad says, cutting me off. "You haven't even tried it yet."

"But—"

He ignores me, rotating my arm and then gesturing to a row of buttons on my forearm. "We'll start with a small flame. Push the purple button."

Hoo boy. I really don't want this thing on me, but Dad's not going to take no for an answer, so I wince and slowly push the purple button.

A thirty-foot orange jet shoots from my palm, engulfing a nearby workbench in flames.

"**WHOA!**" we both yell. Barely avoiding incineration, Dad grabs my arm and jabs at the controls. Eventually, he hits the button that makes the flame disappear, but by then he's melted the beakers, flasks, and Bunsen burners into slag.

"Dad! How is that a small flame?"

"You hit the wrong button. I said hit the purple button. Purple!" He points at a button that's clearly not purple.

Ugh.

It's bad enough Dad won't admit he's colorblind. But why does he insist on color-coding the controls of the weapons he designs? Honestly, it's a miracle this hollowed-out volcano we call home didn't blow up years ago.

"Now let's try this again. Push the purple button!"

I roll my eyes and then squint at the control panel. Let's see, how did it go again? When Dad says "purple," he actually means...

I push the blue button, and fire shoots from my open palm. This time, the flame is only six inches long. I breathe a sigh of relief. Much better. I raise my hand and watch the orange flame dance around. While the last one was angry and explosive, this one seems...cute, almost.

Slowly, I curl my fingers, and as I do, the flame shrinks. When I make a fist, the flame goes out. When I open my hand, **FOOMF!** It's back, brighter than ever.

A smile tugs at the corners of my mouth. I can't help it. Sure, it's horribly dangerous. Sure, it's horrendously irresponsible. But I have to admit this thing is kind of cool.

"See? What did I tell you? You like it!" Dad goes back to stroking his goatee.

Reluctantly, I nod. "You were right. I do like it."

"Ha," he says, looking triumphant.

I close my hand, and the flame retreats into the device again. "Now, how do I turn it off?"

"Green button, obviously."

"Yeah. Obviously," I mumble, and hit the yellow button. The fire goes out, and the device turns off.

With the threat of incineration gone, Dad jogs over to the smoldering wreckage of his workbench to assess the damage. I follow him, wrinkling my nose at the smells of melted plastic and burned wood. "Oh no, Dad! Your bio-weapons station!" We've managed to turn it into a pile of slag and glass.

Dad shakes his head. "No, no. That's over there." He gestures toward an identical-looking workbench. "I was using this area to brew my coffee."

I wrinkle my eyebrows. "Umm, Dad? Don't you think it's kind of a bad idea for a bio-weapons station and a coffee station to be so close to each other?"

Dad looks over at me. "Bad idea? Why would that be a bad idea?"

"Uh...never mind."

Dad rocks back and forth on his heels. "What do you think of your present?"

In my head, I see him standing on a dock, holding a rod and a tackle box. He's just fishing for praise.

"I—I—" What does someone say when they get a deadly weapon for their birthday? I'll think of you whenever I burn something? "Why did you decide to make me a flamethrower?"

"Well, Fiona," Dad says, putting a hand on my shoulder, "I think there's an age in every young girl's life where they need to be able to incinerate whatever they want, wherever they want, whenever they want."

"What?" I sputter. "What age is that?"

Dad just shrugs. "How old are you again? Fourteen?"

"Thirteen!"

"Well, thirteen then. That's the right age for a flamethrower."

"Right." I sigh, blowing my bangs out of my eyes. I don't know why I expected a non-insane answer for such a clearly insane gift. "Can you help me take it off?"

"You're not supposed to take it off."

I blink. "What?"

"I designed it so it wouldn't restrict any movement you'd need for everyday life. There's really no reason you'll ever need to take it off."

"But—" I start to protest. "So I'm supposed to just walk around with this thing on all the time?"

"Yes."

"Even when I'm at school?"

"Yeah, why not?"

"Dad, no." I put my hands on my hips, as I always do when I'm being adamant about something. Only this time, I accidentally punch my side with my now-metallic right hand. A whimper catches in my throat. Ow. That's gonna bruise. "Everyone at school already believes I'm a freak! Don't you think this will just make it worse?"

"No. Actually, I think it'll help. Think of how popular you'll be now. Kids like fire, right?"

"No!" I sputter again. "Stuff like this is how I got into the situation I'm in."

"What situation?"

"The other kids think I'm a freak because of you!"

"Me?" Dad stares at me. "What did I do?"

What did he do? Is he seriously asking that? "I ride to school in a helicopter, I live in a giant hollowed-out volcano, and my dad is Manson Ng, evil super-villain extraordinaire, who regularly terrorizes the town just to show he can. And let's see…" I start counting off my black, metallic fingers. "You melted the mayor's car last summer with a giant laser—"

"He was parked in my spot!"

"—you started an earthquake just to see how prepared the town was for emergencies—"

"That was a public service!"

"—and you were just on the news last week for setting the town's fire station on fire and then cackling manically as it burned to the ground!"

"I was not cackling—"

"You were totally cackling!"

"No, I wasn't."

"Yes, you were."

"It. Was. Funny!" he says, emphasizing each word as if somehow this makes them make sense. "The fire station was on fire, and they couldn't put it out because the fire station was on fire!"

I open my mouth to tell him how dumb that sounded, but then I think about it. Okay, that is actually kind of funny.

"You see? You see?" He jabs a finger at the giggle I'm trying to suppress. "I would like to state, right here, right now, how simultaneously awesome and hilarious Operation Flaming Irony was. When you get older, and you become a super-villain yourself, you'll understand why we cackle so much."

I glare at him. Not this again. "Dad, I told you. I don't want to be a super-villain."

"Of course you do. Don't be silly."

"But—"

"Fiona, we've discussed this. You're taking over the family business when you grow up. You said that's what you wanted to do."

"No I didn't. That's what you want me to do. I never said that's what I want to do."

"Stop being foolish. You'll be a super-villain, just like me, and that's final!"

Ugh. Can we not have this fight again? On my birthday no less? "Dad," I say, as forcefully as I can. I put my hands on my hips, carefully avoiding the bruise forming on my side. "I. Don't. Want. To. Be. A. Super. Villain! I want to have a normal career. I want to go to college and become a doctor and go to Africa to help starving children!"

Dad turns beet-red. "A doctor? Africa?" He spits each word to the floor, as if they are chunks of bitter melon dipped in disappointment sauce. "Why don't you just stab a knife into my heart?"

I rub my temples, trying to push back the headache that's starting to form.

"Help starving children. Pah!" He looks nauseated. "You know what? Just go ahead and stab me. Just stab a dagger into my heart right now. Do you still have that sword I gave you?"

"Dad, stop being so melodramatic."

"Melodramatic? Me?"

"Sir." A red-clad henchman holding a cardboard box pokes his head through the doorway. "Sir, your capes just arrived—"

Dad spins to face him. "Not a good time."

"But—"

"Dammit, soldier! Put the capes in the cape closet with the rest of the capes. It's not that hard!"

The henchman shuffles out of the room as Dad turns back to me. "What were we talking about again?"

"Nothing important," I snap. "I should be getting ready to go to school anyway."

"Fine. We can talk about this later."

I scowl, pushing a strand of black hair behind my ear. Hopefully something will distract him by the time I get back, and he'll forget all about it.

I turn to leave, but I remember something. "Dad, you never did answer my question."

"What question?"

"Why the flamethrower? Why now?"

"Like I said, you're at the age where—"

"But you forgot how old I am! So that's not it…"

Dad's anger evaporates, and his eyes dart from side to side.

"What's going on?" I ask, suspicious. "You're lying to me, aren't you?"

"No…I'm not!"

His eyes dart even faster now. He's totally lying.

"Yes, you are." Now it's my turn to shove a finger at him. "What's the real reason?"

"I—uh—" He coughs. "I just wanted to make sure...that in case anything should happen...you can protect yourself."

"Protect myself? From what?"

A muffled thump reverberates throughout the room. It sounds like it came from above us. Then another one, louder this time, strong enough to jolt walls, knock beakers over, and shake the ground. I lose my balance, crashing to the floor as rocks fall from the ceiling, showering us with debris.

Wide-eyed, I look at Dad. He's holding on to a nearby shelf to avoid falling over. "What was that?"

Before Dad can respond, the base's air-raid siren goes off.

"**HOW** many?" Dad barks at the grim-faced soldiers surrounding him.

"We can't get an exact count. Our radar was the first thing they took out. At least a dozen, maybe two." Uncle Tom adjusts his wire-rimmed glasses as he looks at his clipboard.

Uncle Tom is Dad's second-in-command. They've known each other since before I was born, and even though he's not really my uncle, Dad considers him part of the family. I do too. Without a doubt, he's the second-smartest person I've ever known. Dad being the first, of course.

"Jade…" Dad says, seething.

Jade is another super-villain, who lives in an abandoned Air Force base nearby. For as long as I've known her, there have been problems between our two families, but this? We've never attacked each other so openly. Heck, I even know Jade's daughter Ruby from school. She and I have a bit of a love-hate relationship. Except, you know, without the love.

"Sir!" Major Morton joins us from the corridor. Jim Morton is the commander of our family's private army. He wears an eye patch and scowls a lot, and although I've known him forever, he still intimidates me. "All units are combat ready."

"Good," Dad says, and then turns to Uncle Tom. "What's our tactical situation?"

"Bad. Our missiles can't seem to lock on for some reason and their planes are too fast for our AA guns."

"Damn it," Dad says under his breath.

I'm a little taken aback by Dad's swearing, but the thing about Dad is he's a completely different person in a crisis. Under normal circumstances, he can be silly, jokey, and even goofy. But in a crisis, he barks orders like a five-star general.

A shriek fills the air, and I look up. A white dive-bomber is screaming toward us through the opening of our volcano-base, its engines getting louder and louder.

"Down!" Major Morton yells, and we all dive for cover. The dive-bomber detonates its payload against the inner wall of the volcano, raining debris on everyone. Had it been dropped fifty yards to the right, we'd all be dead.

"I hate that sound," I mutter through clenched teeth. Judging by how shaken everyone looks, I'm not the only one.

"Close the top. Now!" Dad shouts into a radio, and the bombproof plate slowly slides shut over our volcano home. "Jim!"

Major Morton turns to Dad. "Sir?"

"Get to the helicopter bay and prepare to repel invaders."

Invaders? We're being invaded? This is turning out to be the worst birthday ever.

Major Morton doesn't seem fazed. "Yes, sir!" He nods confidently, slinging his rifle over his shoulder before running off. His feet clomp on the metal floor.

"Fiona," Dad says, pulling me along. "I need you to get to safety."

Dad drags me to the emergency elevator, and my eyes go wide with panic even before Dad inserts his key into the control panel.

"Dad, no." I shake my head, desperately. "Please, not that—"

Dad bends down so he's eye-to-eye with me. "Honey, you have to."

"But I want to stay with you."

He shakes his head. "It's too dangerous. Uncle Tom and I are going to be in the control room directing our defenses, but if something goes wrong..." Dad pauses. "I need you to be safe in the escape pod."

The red elevator opens, and Dad gently pushes me in. He turns his key and the doors start to close, but at the last moment I shove my metallic arm between them.

"Dad—I—I love you." A lump grows in my throat. It isn't fair. This is supposed to be my birthday. This is supposed to be a happy day.

"I love you, too, sweetheart. We'll be okay, I promise." He smiles at me one last time and turns his key again. The doors slide shut, and the elevator descends.

I wipe the wetness from my eyes with my sleeve. Why did this have to happen today, of all days? Most people get to spend their birthdays eating cake and having parties. But I get to spend my birthday hiding.

I hate the stupid escape pod. It's basically a coffin mounted on a giant cannon, and it's barely big enough for me. I'm supposed to strap myself in and, if things get really bad out there, there's a button in the escape pod that sends me blasting to "safety." I tested it once when I was six; by the time they pulled me out of the ocean, I was so motion-sick I couldn't stand for a week. Stupid escape pod.

Why is Jade attacking us, anyway? The three super-villain families have been scrapping for as long as I remember, but we usually focus on the thwarting of evil plans versus actual fighting. One time Jade pulled off a daylight robbery on a Chilean gold mine, only to find we had already stolen all the gold nuggets and replaced them with gold-painted horse manure. That's the kind of stuff we usually did to each other. But this is a whole other ball game.

I just wanted to make sure you could protect yourself.

Dad's words echo in my head, and I reach into my pocket to fish out my new lighter. Protect myself? Is this what he meant?

BOOM!

Something explodes up top, sending shock waves through the base. The elevator lurches to a stop and I crash to the floor, sending my lighter clattering against the metal. The lights blink out.

Crap.

I feel around in the darkness, fighting a rising tide of panic. The enclosed space and the stifling heat make me want to scream. I can't breathe. It's like I'm buried alive.

Finally, I manage to find my lighter, and with shaking fingers I flick it on.

The dark shrinks back, fleeing from the tiny flame, and gradually my dread disappears. But then I see the smoke.

I cough, the fumes clinging to my throat like an unwelcome houseguest clings to the remote. I need to get out of here. Now.

I yank open a control panel and peer into a mass of wires, but all I see are red lights, flashing angrily.

I jab several buttons but nothing happens. Great. What the heck do I do now?

The smoke gets thicker and I spin around, scanning the tiny elevator for…something. Anything. There has to be a way out of here.

A glint of metal catches my eye, and I hold my lighter up to it. There's a lever above the door with an "Emergency Release" label stuck to it. I'm pretty sure this counts as an emergency. I grab it and pull.

The elevator door slides open with a clunk, and I can see the top half of a second set of metal doors. I have no idea how deep I am or what lies on the other side, but it will beat being stuck. I jam my metallic fingers between the panels and, with a bit of grunting, I wrench them open.

The only light comes from red emergency lights mounted on the walls, and it's mostly obscured by the smoke.

I slide out, praying the elevator doesn't plummet and slice me in half. Luckily, I emerge into the maze of unmarked corridors in one piece.

Where am I?

There are no signs, maps, or directions. Which makes sense, since no one would put signs up in their own house, but then again, most people's houses probably don't burp sulfur, as mine does.

These sublevels are where mundane things like generators and water pumps are kept. I've never had a reason to come down here, since I don't know how to fix a generator. But now I really wish I did.

I wander until I come upon a four-way intersection. Each direction seems to stretch into smoky infinity.

I'm paralyzed by indecision, but as I'm about to give up, I spot a tall figure through the smoke. I run toward him.

"Hey!" I yell, waving my arms.

A man turns around. He's wearing dark goggles, a grey hood, and a gas mask that makes him sound like Darth Vader every time he breathes. With a growing sense of horror, I realize he's not one of ours.

He grabs my shoulder and slams me into the concrete wall. When I open my mouth to scream, he shoves a gun into my face.

The world slows as I stare down the barrel of his gun. Nothing else matters. All I can see are the swirling grooves etched into the barrel. Beads of sweat trickle down my forehead, and my heart jackhammers in my chest. I count my heartbeats, wondering which one will be my last.

"Well, hello there," the masked man says. His voice sounds hollow and distant even though he's right there in front of me. "Look who I've found."

I look around desperately, but all I see (besides the man in the gas mask) is smoke, smoke, and more smoke. Nobody's coming to rescue me. Nobody knows I need rescuing.

But that doesn't mean we're alone. The masked man turns to his right and gestures broadly. "Over here! I've got the girl!"

Loud feet pound the concrete like rampaging buffalo. Flashlight beams pierce the smoke, getting closer by the second.

I'm trapped. Helpless. And nobody knows I'm down here. With no other options left, I do the only thing I can think of.

I stomp on the masked man's foot.

He yelps, and as his grip loosens I break free and take off.

I was never much of a track star, but I feel like I'm flying through the air. After fishing my lighter out of my pocket, I try desperately to light it, but my fingers are shaking so hard I can't. My heart's going a mile a minute, and my feet are going about ten times that. I'm running so quickly I barely notice something hot flash past, shattering one of the emergency bulbs lining the hallway.

I whip my head around without breaking stride, trying to glimpse what's behind me. The footsteps grow louder, and flashlights, hungry for targets, search the smoke. They're getting closer. But I don't care. I'm never going to let them catch me.

Then I slam right into something large.

Shrieking, I bounce off a mountain of muscle and crash painfully to the concrete. I look up at my captor, expecting to see another gray mask. But instead, I see…an eyepatch.

I've found Major Morton.

I have no idea what he's doing down here, or how I managed to run into him, but I've never been happier to see that eyepatch in my whole life. I would jump up and hug him, but Major Morton's not much of a hugger. Besides, he has other plans.

Wordlessly, he takes one look at me, then another at the flashlights behind me. All it takes is a split second for him to size up the situation. When the split second's over, he's already made up his mind about how to take care of things.

Major Morton takes a thick disk, like a puck, out of his vest and tosses it down the hallway toward the advancing boots. Then he grabs my metallic wrist and pulls me to my feet and into a nearby supply closet. For a hulking guy, he's surprisingly fast, and I almost trip over my own feet.

For a second, I'm not sure what his plan is. Why would we corner ourselves in a closet? Then he flips down his helmet headset to reveal a clear screen over his eye.

I recognize the device from Dad's lab. It's a universal headset, capable of connecting to any of the gadgets he's built. Anything with a camera, really.

Like the puck-shaped explosive Major Morton just threw down the hall.

Patiently, he waits until his screen fills with the image of my almost-captor's boots, and then he hits a button.

The explosion sends cleaning supplies careening off the shelves. Major Morton whips open the door, leans out, and starts blasting his rifle.

I grit my teeth. I hate guns. I absolutely hate them. Especially the ones our soldiers carry. They're massive, almost as big as I am. Major Morton often brags that a single one of our soldiers carries enough firepower to take down a tank, and right now, I completely believe it. Every shot is like a cannon going off next to my head. And under normal circumstances, I would yell at him for firing that thing so close to me. But today is about as far from normal circumstances as you can possibly get.

So I just cover my ears with my hands. My lighter clatters to the floor as I try to keep my teeth from rattling out of my skull and my wits from rattling out of my mind. I just think I'm getting the hang of things when a paint can bounces painfully off my head.

But it's not the paint can that stuns me. It's the silence. Absolute silence.

Major Morton turns back to me as he reloads his rifle. "Aren't you supposed to be strapped to a cannon somewhere?"

I chuckle, rubbing the bump on my head. "The elevator broke."

"The one time we needed that stupid thing to work." He rolls his eye. "I guess you'd better come with me, then. Wouldn't want you running into any more trouble, now, would we?"

I shake my head.

Major Morton leans out, peering into the hallway. Confident the coast is clear, he turns back to me. "Stay close behind me. If anything happens, you hit the ground. And if I tell you to do something, you do it. Got it?"

I nod, adrenaline coursing through me. As I'm getting ready to move, I notice my lighter, still lying on the ground. I have just enough time to scoop it up and stuff it back into my skirt pocket before Major Morton says, "Let's go."

He brings his rifle to his shoulder, scanning for targets as we walk through the smoke together. My heart races, and every so often I glance behind me, expecting someone to start shooting at us again, but nobody does.

It feels like an eternity, but after countless corridors, a light cuts through the smoke. Part of me wants to make a break for it, but Major Morton remains cautious.

We walk toward the light cautiously, his gun up and ready to fire. Finally, we break through the smoke together and walk into the light—to find a hundred guns aimed right at our heads.

There's an army waiting for us.

Fortunately, it's our army.

"Major. Glad you could join us." The speaker has a thick New York accent, and smiles as he offers an outstretched hand.

"Sergeant, good to see you." Major Morton smiles back, gripping the sergeant's hand. "How are we doing?"

We're in the helicopter bay. It's full of our soldiers, and some of Jade's as well. But with their hands bound behind their backs, they don't look nearly as scary anymore. Our men stand guard over them, glaring suspiciously.

"These guys aren't half-bad in the air, but they're absolutely terrible on the ground. Half of them got smoked in the initial landing, and the other half ran off with their tails between their legs. A few are scattered around the base, but nothing we can't handle without breaking a sweat."

"That's what happens when you tangle with the Storm Troopers," Major Morton says, smirking.

The sergeant smirks back. "Absolutely."

Storm Troopers. I came up with that name years ago, and it was supposed to be a joke. You know, the faceless henchmen of the Galactic Empire from Star Wars? But over the years the name stuck. They started calling each other that. They even became proud of that name, and I never understood why. Until now.

"Uh-huh. Yeah, she's fine." Major Morton talks into his headset. "Roger that." He turns to me. "Kiddo, it looks like this is where we part ways. I just spoke to your dad, and he wants you on a chopper and out of harm's way pronto."

"Okay." I nod, my heartbeat still pounding in my ears. "At least I don't have to be in an escape pod anymore."

Major Morton chuckles. "Lucky you."

"What are you going to do?" I ask.

"Me? I've still got some cleaning up. You know, taking out the rest of the trash."

"You were awesome back there, Major."

"I know. Imagine if I had both my eyes!" He grins, winking his good eye at me. "Hey, isn't it your birthday today?"

I smile, nodding.

"Well, happy birthday!"

I shrug. "I guess…"

"Pretty exciting, huh?"

"I'll say. I've never been shot at before."

"Well, you know what they say. Everyone remembers their first time, right?"

I laugh. The joke is probably a little inappropriate for a thirteen-year-old, but after everything I've been through, I'm not sure what "appropriate" is anymore. "How are you so okay with it?"

Major Morton shrugs. "We're Storm Troopers. We're supposed to get shot at."

With that, he brings his rifle up to his shoulder. "Squad One! On me!" He jogs back into the tunnels, into the smoke and gunfire. I watch him go, and in all the years I've known him, I've never seen him this happy before.

The whir of the helicopter's accelerating blades fills the air, and I strap myself into one of the passenger seats. The chopper is painted red and black and, like everything else in our family arsenal, custom designed by Dad. Its armor is strong enough to shrug off bullets without even a scratch, and it has enough missiles and rockets attached to its side to level a skyscraper.

It's also my ride to school every day.

We lift off as I slide one of the big headsets over my ears, positioning the microphone so I can communicate with the pilot.

"Exciting day, huh?" Mike's radio-filtered voice blares.

"Yeah, I'll say."

"All right. Before we go, Control's asked me to do a couple fly-arounds and call in a damage report, so just sit tight, okay?"

"Sure." I'm in no hurry.

We gain some altitude and then gently bank left to do some slow, lazy circles around the base. When we do, I gasp at the extent of the damage.

Our enemies have bombed our volcano home into the Stone Age. Fires rage across the mountain, and thick plumes of smoke stand in the sky like black obelisks. Fire crews battle the blazes, spraying white powder that does little to stanch the flames. Our radar dish lies in charred pieces on the rocky shores below, and the few pockets of trees that once grew along the sides are blown to smithereens. Noticeably absent is any wreckage from their aircraft. I don't think we downed a single one.

Oh well. They beat us in the air, but we beat them on the ground.

As Mike radios in his damage report, I notice the one thing that seems to have escaped unharmed—the steel slab over the top of the volcano. Dad installed it last summer instead of building me the pool I wanted. At the time I was peeved, but right now I'm so glad he didn't cave.

"Okay, we're done here. We can go," says Mike.

"Great."

"So, where to, little lady?"

I look up. "Do I have to pick?"

"My orders are to evacuate you, but they don't specify where. Lady's choice, it seems…"

"Uh... I don't..." Great, it's happening again. I'm lost in the tunnels, staring down all the endless corridors, endless choices, frozen in place.

"Should we go to the missile silo?" Mike suggests helpfully.

"No, not the silo." I hate that place. Too dank.

"The bomb shelter?"

"Nah..." I hate that place even more. No Internet.

Shaking my head in frustration, I brush some dirt off my school uniform. I'm still wearing the white blouse and red pleated skirt from this morning. Except now they're more soot-colored than white and red. Staring at the letters "NV" embroidered on the logo patch of my skirt, I suddenly realize where I want to go.

"Take me to school."

Mike seems taken aback. "School? Really?"

"This has been a really weird day. I just...I could just use some normal right now."

Mike thinks about it and then shrugs. "Okay. School it is."

They call us "The Kingpins." Me, Ruby, and Jai. We're schoolmates, and our parents are... Well, let's just say they all picked a similar, non-traditional career path. Ruby's family is rumored to have one of the largest and most advanced private air forces in the entire world. Well, it was a rumor, anyway, up until this morning. And Jai? You might say he's "of no fixed address," because Jai lives on a battleship. He regularly brags that his family's got the biggest guns of anyone, and he's probably right. His dad goes by "The Captain," so I guess my dad's not the only one with a bit of flair for melodrama. Just in case that wasn't complicated enough, The Families are all sworn enemies of each other. So that's my life. That's my normal.

I'm not sure who came up with the name The Kingpins, but somehow it stuck, and I can see why. It makes the three of us sound mysterious—dangerous, even. But all it means is that anytime anyone sees us coming, they dive for cover. They think that, because The Families are sworn enemies at any given moment, the three of us will suddenly freak out and attack each other.

I can tell Jai doesn't mind the name. Being a Kingpin makes him terrifying, and he likes that. A little too much, actually. And Ruby, I can never really tell what she's thinking. Then there's me. I try to be nice and act like a regular person. But no matter how hard I try, every time someone walks by me in the hall, they never want to get close. To them, I'll always be a Kingpin.

I arrive during our lunch break, and students mill around in the halls, laughing and talking. But when they see me they scatter like rats. Within seconds the hallway is deserted. Sighing, I head toward my locker.

"But I already gave you my lunch money!" a high-pitched voice squeaks from up ahead.

I push open the hallway doors and find Jai wrestling his locker door shut.

"Jai, what are you doing?"

He whirls around, scowling. "Why don't you mind your own busine—" he starts to say, but stops when he sees me.

Jai has always been a weird juxtaposition of colors—jet-black hair, cocoa-brown skin, sky-blue eyes, and alabaster teeth. I've always wondered how it's possible to get all those colors into one person.

"Oh. Hey, Sparky!" Jai beams at me, his smile lighting up his entire face.

Ugh. Jai's been calling me "Sparky" ever since grade school. Apparently, whenever I get mad at him (which happens a lot), I get all red, twitchy, and, according to Jai, "have sparks shooting out of my ears." I can shoot way more than sparks now, I remind myself as I flex my metallic fingers.

"What's wrong?" He cocks his head. "You look mad enough to set off an entire fireworks factory."

"Ugh. Today's the worst day ever."

Jai closes his locker, comes over, and wraps a brotherly arm around my shoulders. "Tell me what happened."

I tell him about the air raid and the invasion. I tell him about the henchman who almost caught me and how Major Morton rescued me from certain death at the last minute. I blast him with every miserable detail of my entire morning, and it isn't until it's all out that I notice his lack of reaction.

I glower at him. "You know all this already, don't you?"

"Sorry." Jai shrugs. "There's not a lot our radar doesn't see."

"So why didn't you say anything?"

"Because talking about it always makes you feel better."

I'm about to make some snappy comeback when I realize he's right. Letting it off my chest did make me feel better.

There aren't a whole lot of people in my life I can really talk to about stuff like this. Most of our classmates would be surprised to learn that Jai is actually not the psychopath out of the three of us. Most people think he's a bully—a muscle-bound jerk. The Nightmare of New Valley Middle School. However, around me, he's a completely different person. He's someone to hang out with, someone to confide in. He's my friend—my only friend.

I hear someone whimper inside the locker, and instantly I'm reminded why he's my only friend.

I narrow my eyes. "Jai, are you bullying the other kids again?"

"No!" he responds, a little too fast.

My eye-narrowing turns into a full-on death glare.

He shifts his gaze. "Maybe."

I sigh, shoving him out of the way with my metallic elbow. When I open the locker, a skinny kid wearing Lennon glasses spills out. He blinks at the sudden light and then locks eyes with Jai, and before I can say, "Are you okay?" he shoots down the hall like an over-caffeinated bat out of hell.

"I wish you'd stop doing that," I say, for the thousandth time.

"And I wish you would stop letting kids out of lockers," he says. "It just makes more work for me later when I have to stuff them back in."

"Jai. I'm serious." I put my hands on my hips, accidentally punching the earlier bruise. "It makes us all look like bad guys."

He gives me a look of pure disbelief. "Um, Sparky? I've got a news flash for you." He comes closer, until his face is only inches from mine. "We…are…the…bad…guys. I've accepted it. When are you going to?"

"I…I just…" I throw up my hands. "I just want to fit in, Jai. I want to be normal."

"I know. But we're not normal, Sparky, and we never will be. You're supposed to be smart. Why can't you see that?"

I roll my eyes. "Just promise me you'll stop bullying the other kids, okay? For me?"

"Fine." Jai shrugs.

But then I hear another whimper from the locker beside him. And a cough from a few lockers away.

I turn toward him. I don't need to say a single word. Accusations fly out of my eyes like laser beams.

Jai shrugs sheepishly. "Err…ah…starting tomorrow?"

With mental sparks shooting out of my head, I open each locker and let each kid out. They scurry into the hallway without a backward glance. No one even stops to thank me. To them, I'm just another Kingpin, like Jai.

"Jai, you suck!" I punch him in the arm as I've done thousands of times. Only this time, my metallic hand slams into him with a painful-sounding clunk.

"Ow!" Jai recoils. "What the heck is that thing? A bionic arm?" I look down at my black metal fist. Whoops. "That really hurt!"

"Sorry. I'm still getting used to it."

Jai rubs his shoulder. I can tell his ego is more bruised than his arm. Jeez. This thing is harder than I thought. I'm going to have to be more careful with it.

Finally he turns his attention to me. "Why did you come back, anyway?"

"Uh, because I go to school here?"

"No, what I mean is…" His hands circle in the air, searching for the right words. "We saw the attack this morning on our radar, as it was happening. This wasn't Jade just sending your family a message. She threw everything she had at you. She tried to kill you."

"I know. I was there."

"So, aren't you worried?"

I furrow my brow. "Worried? About what?"

"Ruby! Aren't you worried she'll try to, you know, finish the job?"

I open my mouth, but nothing comes out. To be honest, the thought hasn't crossed my mind. I've known Ruby almost as long as I've known Jai, and even though she's not the friendliest person in the world, would she actually beat me to a pulp if her parents told her to? I think about it and figure, no. No way.

But then again, there's a first time for everything.

"We're off-limits," I tell Jai, repeating something our parents always told us growing up. No matter what goes on among The Families, nobody would ever use the kids against each other. That's the agreement.

Jai shakes his head. "No, we were off-limits. Until this morning. I don't like it."

"How do you think I feel? At least your breakfast didn't come with a side order of dive bombers."

Jai ignores me and starts pacing, something I've never seen him do before. This must really bother him. "The Families have their problems, but it's never been like this. I mean, foiling each other's evil plans, that's one thing. But this? A direct attack? Something's different. Something's changed."

"What do you think it is?"

Jai shrugs.

An electronic chime sounds over the loudspeaker, and Jai and I exchange glances.

"I guess I have to go."

"Right." Jai rolls his eyes at me. "Better run off to class. Wouldn't want to be late and have absolutely nothing happen."

"It makes me feel normal."

Jai snorts. "Normal gets stuffed into lockers."

"So what are you saying? You going to stuff me in a locker?"

"No way. You're my Sparky! And besides." Jai grins at me while rubbing the bruise forming on his shoulder. "You've got a mean right hook."

I laugh. "Later, Jai."

But as I'm about to leave, he says, "Hey, Sparky."

I turn around. "What?"

"You know, things are just going to get more dangerous from here on out. The fighting among The Families, I mean. It's going to get worse."

I pause. "Yeah, probably."

Jai clears his throat. "Just…watch your back, okay?"

I flex my metallic fingers. "Always."

The students are already seated when I burst into Ms. Harding's math class. Everyone looks up from their notes when the door slams behind me. "Sorry I'm late."

Ms. Harding stops scribbling equations on the board. "If you're going to interrupt the class at least—" She brushes away the wisp of grey hair covering her eyes and turns, seeing me. "Oh. Miss. Fiona. Well, I'm…ah…I'm sure you had a good reason. Why don't you take your seat?"

I look up at the clock. "But I'm over ten minutes late. Aren't you going to give me a detention?"

"Oh, no, no, no." She shakes her head. "The detention room is…ah…being renovated today, so no detentions for anyone. You're in luck!"

I gape in confusion. I passed by that room on the way here, and I don't remember seeing any renovations. She has to be making that up. Then again, I guess being a Kingpin does have some minor advantages. I sink quietly into my seat in the front row.

Ms. Harding turns back toward the board. "As I was saying, to calculate the surface area of a cylinder, you simply apply the following equation…"

I breathe a sigh of relief. Good, I didn't miss anything important. Surface area of a cylinder? I've had that homework done for weeks now.

The door flies open with a bang and everyone jumps. Especially me.

Cue ominous music!

No, no, I'm kidding. Don't cue ominous music. If Ruby could get ominous music to play every time she entered a room, I'm pretty sure her head would grow so big she'd fall over.

For such a tiny person, each step she takes seems to pound the ground into submission. Her shiny black combat boots have silver skull buckles that jangle as she walks. She's wearing a black leather mini-skirt and a lacy black corset. In fact, everything she has on is black, making her skin look even paler than usual.

Ruby's not her real name. Nobody knows her real name, or the names of anyone in her family. All we know are their call signs. She comes from a family of pilots. Her mom's a pilot, her dad's a pilot, and, from what little information our spies uncovered, she's a pretty freaking good pilot herself. The thing about pilots is once a call sign sticks, it sticks hard. They use it for everything. Her dad's call sign is Hawk because he has the "eyes of a hawk." Her mom's call sign is Jade, probably because of how insanely rich she is. And Ruby? Her call sign's because of her eyes. Ruby's albino, so her skin and hair are white. Everything about her is ivory-white, except her eyes. They're ruby red.

Unlike me, Ruby doesn't even try to care that she's fifteen minutes late. She returns Ms. Harding's gaze with a fiery stare of her own. "What are you looking at?"

Ms. Harding quickly turns back to her whiteboard, while Ruby takes her seat, way at the back of the class. However, as she walks down the aisle, she spots me and stops in her tracks. For a second I wonder why she's just standing there staring at me. Then suddenly I understand.

She wasn't expecting to see me again.

Slowly, she walks to her seat, glaring at me the entire way.

"Now then." Ms. Harding clears her throat. "The moment you've all been waiting for, I'm sure. Your tests have been graded, so if you'd like to come up to the front, you can have them back."

Everyone rushes up to Ms. Harding's desk, pushing and shoving. I'm right there with them, and for a few precious seconds, the other students forget who I am. I'm one of them, an anonymous uniform in the crowd. I can't remember the last time I felt so normal.

I glance at Ruby—the only one who isn't part of the crowd. She sits at her desk, playing with her phone, as if she couldn't care less about her grade.

I grab my paper and break into a wide smile. I got 100! I got 100!

Finally, something's going my way today.

Still beaming, I take my seat, along with everyone else, and read over my test. But as my eyes scan the page, my smile disappears. Something doesn't add up. Literally.

"No way," I say a little too loudly.

"Is there a problem, Miss Fiona?" Ms. Harding looks up.

"There's a mistake on my test!"

"What do you mean?" she replies, wiping her palms along the sides of her long black skirt. "Didn't you get a perfect score?"

I cross the short distance between our desks and point to question three.

"I made a mistake here. The first term of this polynomial is supposed to be multiplied by four. I multiplied by three."

"But your underlying work was correct, so I let it slide."

I blink, confused. "But it's wrong. Don't you want to re-mark it?"

"No." She shakes her head, a little too emphatically. "The marks are final, Miss Fiona. I couldn't change them even if I wanted to."

Couldn't change them even if she... What is she talking about? I look over at Ruby's test, still sitting on Ms. Harding's desk from where Ruby didn't pick it up. It's also marked 100. "Look," I point. "Ruby put down a different answer for this question, and yet we both got 100!"

"Well...the questions are open to interpretation..." Ms. Harding says, beads of sweat forming on her forehead.

"Open to interpretation? This is math class. These are numbers. We can't both be right!"

"Look," she puts her hands up defensively. "I don't want any trouble."

Only then do I notice the splint wrapped around her left pinkie. "What happened to your hand?"

Ms. Harding shoves her injured hand under her desk. "N-nothing. It was an accident." Her eyes dart to the floor, and her other hand rests on the desk, shaking noticeably. After a few seconds, she looks up, and we exchange glances. Almost imperceptibly, her nervous gaze flickers behind me.

Slowly, I turn around. In the back of the room, Ruby stops texting and flicks those blood-red eyes up at the two of us. For a split second, a smile starts to form on her lips, but then it's gone, and she goes back to playing with her phone.

The class phone rings, causing Ms. Harding to jump. With trembling hands, she picks up the receiver.

"Y-yes? Uh-huh? Okay, I'll be right there."

She stands up, "Class, I need to speak with the Principal about something. Please work on questions one to five on page seventeen while I'm gone." She straightens her blouse and tries to exit the classroom with her head held high, but a soft sob escapes her.

From the back of the class, Ruby snaps her phone shut and looks up at me. "That was amusing. Still trying to be normal, I see?"

"You didn't have to do that."

"Do what?" she replies, all innocent-like. I want to smack her. "What's that thing on your arm? Another one of your dad's toys?"

I don't answer, my blood boiling.

"He's got a lot of toys in that volcano lair of his. So I hear."

I still don't answer. There's little I can say right now that wouldn't be a string of curse words.

"Well, if you're not going to say anything, why don't you sit back down? This one-sided conversation's boring."

Something snaps inside me. "Why don't you shut up and make me, Ruby?"

Everyone gasps. Nobody has ever, ever spoken to a Kingpin like that. Everybody knows that anyone who does won't live to see another sunrise. Then again, I'm not just anyone, am I? I'm a Kingpin too.

Now I've got Ruby's attention. "Well, well, well. Fiona grows a backbone. When did this happen?"

I'm seething. If sparks literally shot out of my ears right now, I wouldn't even blink.

"To be honest," she continues, "I wasn't expecting to see you today."

"You weren't expecting to see me today?" I shoot back through gritted teeth. "Or you weren't expecting to see me alive?"

The tension is so thick it feels like I'm back in the tunnels again.

"That's not what I meant." She brushes her whiter-than-white bangs out of her eyes. "Come on now, do you think that little of me? We've known each other since we were kids. Actually, to be honest, I'm glad you're here. I've got something for you."

Ruby reaches into her backpack, and the entire classroom panics. Kids dive for cover under their desks. One girl crumples into a corner and starts sobbing uncontrollably.

I reach for my lighter. Is this it? Is this actually going to happen?

Smirking, apparently amused by everybody's reactions, Ruby slowly withdraws her hand from her backpack to reveal…a rock. The classroom collectively sighs.

"Wow, everyone sure is jumpy today." She turns to me and glances at the lighter in my hand. "And since when do you smoke?"

I flick my birthday gift closed and slide it back into my pocket. "I don't—"

"So, aren't you going to ask me what this is?"

"No, but I have a feeling you're going to tell me anyway."

"It's from your volcano." She strokes it like a kitten. "Mom gave this to me. You know how I am about collecting stuff, so now I get to have a piece of your home. Fun, huh?"

The urge to smack her is getting harder to contain. The only thing stopping me is the thought of what else she might have in that backpack.

"You know, I heard you didn't manage to down a single one of our planes."

I nod. "That's true. We didn't. Your pilots are very good."

Ruby smiles. "Yes, they are."

"Your foot soldiers, on the other hand, not so much."

Now it's her turn to glare at me. "What?"

What was it the Sergeant said to Major Morton? "We smoked half of them in the first few minutes, and the other half got back in their helicopters and flew off with their tails between their legs." Yeah, that was it.

She grits her insanely white teeth. "You're lying."

"I guess what I said wasn't entirely accurate. Some of them we captured. They're in our prison cells. I'm sure they'll tell us all sorts of interesting things." I flick a piece of lint off my white blouse. "Maybe some of them will get their fingers broken. After all, accidents happen..."

Ruby practically has steam wafting out of her ears. "You're lying! We didn't lose any soldiers."

I blink. "You don't know, do you?"

"What are you talking about? Know what?"

"What actually happened."

"I know we beat the crap out of you."

"Yeah," I scoff. "Of course you did." I lick my lips, savoring the moment. "But then again, if that were true, why am I still alive?"

Ruby is livid. I can tell because her face goes from bone-white to tomato-red in two seconds. Apparently, when albinos blush, they blush hard.

"Did you actually count them, Ruby?" I continue, grinding salt into her wounds. "The ones that came back? Did you count them? Because from what I saw, our Storm Troopers just... massacred them. It was pathetic, really. Embarrassing. And I should know. I was there."

I take a step toward her, and she rises from her chair, fists clenched.

But I keep going. "I was unarmed, outnumbered, alone. A pathetic little thirteen-year-old girl, against a squad of soldiers. And they couldn't even pull that off. I'm here and they're not." I shake my head in disbelief. "Who trained those guys? You?"

Ruby grabs the rock off her desk and whips it at my head with everything she's got. Instinctively, I raise my right arm to block, and, with a clang, it bounces harmlessly off the metal.

Ruby rushes toward me. "Let's see how tough you are without Jai."

She slams into me, knocking me to the floor. I twist my body as I fall, and then I'm on top of her. But Ruby kicks with the force of an angry bull, and in an instant she's on top of me.

The other students press up against the wall, wide-eyed. If it were any other two students, they would be forming a circle around us, chanting "Fight! Fight! Fight!" However, with us, nobody's sure who to cheer for, or whether it's even safe to cheer at all. Ruby grabs a handful of my long hair, almost yanking it from my scalp. I scream, and for an instant, I can see that smile forming on Ruby's lips again.

But then I spit, "You fight like a girl," ball my right hand into a fist, and swing.

She flops to the floor, eyes wide and staring, and lies still, as if paralyzed by pain.

I stare at my metallic right arm, hearing Jai's words in my head. I do have a mean right hook!

Ruby tries to get up but I straddle her, raising my metallic fist again. She flinches and struggles to push me off, but I don't budge. I want her to hurt, like she wanted me to hurt this morning, and nothing's going to stop me from getting what I want.

But then, something does stop me.

Ms. Harding is back, with the Principal behind her. Ms. Harding pulls me off Ruby.

"What are you doing?" I yell. "She tried to kill me!"

The Principal is holding Ruby back, and she claws at him like a wolverine. "You think this is over?" she shrieks. "This isn't over!"

As I kick and scream, Ms. Harding drags me outside. Finally, I manage to break loose from her grip and, grabbing her shoulders, I pin her to a nearby locker with the force of my righteous rage. "Why did you stop me?"

Then I notice Tom standing in the hallway.

"Uncle Tom?" I let go of Ms. Harding. "What are you doing here?"

He adjusts his glasses and clears his throat. "Fiona, something's happened..."

"What? What happened?" Nothing good ever comes from the sentence "Something's happened."

"Fiona, I don't quite know how to say this..."

My breath hitches in my throat. It takes everything I have not to run away. Whatever Uncle Tom has to say, I don't want to hear it.

But Uncle Tom drops the bomb on me anyway,

"There's been another attack. While the base's defenses were down, they hit us again, and..." He ahems again. "Your dad is missing."

As I follow Uncle Tom into the control room, I realize this is the first time I've been in here. Monitors, radar screens, and control panels blanket each workstation. Radios and telephones line the lower walls. A massive LCD screen covers one entire upper wall. I can almost see Dad standing in front of it, gloating as he extorts a million dollars from yet another Middle Eastern dictator. However, now the control room is deserted, and all the screens are blank.

"How did this happen?"

Uncle Tom shakes his head. "I'm not sure."

"Aren't you supposed to know everything that's going on?"

He rakes his fingers through his wiry grey hair. I've never seen Uncle Tom like this. He's always calm and in control, but now his red tie is gone, his crisp dress shirt is rumpled, and his normally slicked-back hair is a complete mess. He looks like someone you'd see after a tornado swept away all his possessions.

He gestures helplessly at the blank screens around him. "The security systems were still down from the attack. I was here trying to get everything back online, and your dad was in the tunnels directing repairs. They must have captured him there."

"I don't—" I rub my temples. Now there is no doubt this is the Worst. Birthday. Ever. "I don't understand. How did they get past our Storm Troopers?"

"They were wearing these." Major Morton enters the control room, rifle slung over his shoulder, looking even more grim than usual. He dumps a pile of familiar uniforms on a table. "One of our patrols just found these. They were dressed as our repair crews."

"Dammit," Uncle Tom smacks a nearby desk. "They must have snuck in wearing those after the initial attack."

Major Morton shakes his head. "They didn't have to. They could have been part of the initial invasion. While we fought the main forces, a few of them could have changed into these and then run off to hide somewhere. Nobody would have noticed a repair guy huddled in a supply closet."

Uncle Tom snaps his fingers. "That's why they retreated so quickly."

Major Morton nods. "The retreat was a trick."

"The entire attack was a trick." A shadow passes over Uncle Tom's face.

I collapse into a chair. This is not happening. "Uncle Tom," I look up at him, "what are they going to do to Dad?"

The two of them exchange glances. "Nothing. For now."

"How do you know?"

"Because they left this." Uncle Tom hands me a piece of paper, folded over three times. It looks so plain and innocent, but I know I'm not going to like what it says. Hands shaking, I unfold it.

In big, black, printed letters, the message reads, *We have your father. Deliver the NOVA in 24 hours or we will kill him.*

I bury my head in my hands, suppressing a sob. Today was supposed to be a happy day. I turned thirteen. Dad was going to take me to see a movie. I might have even been able to get him to volunteer with me at the Waikiki soup kitchen afterward. But now? I would give anything to be twelve again.

Wiping the tears from my eyes, I look back at the paper. "What's the NOVA?"

Major Morton rakes his fingers through his hair and looks at Uncle Tom, standing next to him. From this angle, I can't see Major Morton's expression. "I think we're going to have to tell her, Tom."

I sit up straighter. "Tell me what? What is it?"

Uncle Tom clears his throat. "It's a bomb."

"A really powerful bomb," Major Morton adds.

Uncle Tom walks over and plops down into the chair across from me. "It's from back when your father and I used to work together in the Advanced Weapons Research Lab for the Department of Defense. The four of us developed it together."

I furrow my brow. "The four of you?"

"Me, your father...and...uh—" he coughs "—Jade and The Captain."

Wait, what? My head snaps up. My ears hear the words but my brain can't comprehend them. "You all worked together?"

He avoids my eyes and looks down at his hands, like I've caught him with a shameful secret. "Uh, yeah. The four of us...kind of...used to be friends."

Now I know I'm hearing things. "What?"

"This was way before you were born."

"What... How..." How could they possibly have been friends? Jade just tried to kill us! "What the heck happened?"

"That's a...a long story. But anyway, the important thing is, the NOVA is an incredibly powerful bomb that we built together."

My mind reels and every word that comes out is a struggle. "How powerful?"

Uncle Tom scratches the back of his head. "You know the nuclear bombs they dropped on Japan during World War II?"

I cock an eyebrow. "Yeah?"

"It's about a hundred times more powerful than one of them."

"Holy..." I choke on my own words. "Holy crap!"

"It could go up to two hundred times, if the detonation conditions are ideal."

Major Morton fidgets with his rifle. "Basically, if that thing goes off, it kills every single person in the city."

"And that thing's here? In the base?"

Uncle Tom nods. "Right."

"Where, exactly?"

Now Uncle Tom's eyes flicker to the floor. "You know your dad's strange sense of humor?"

I frown at him, not sure I like where's he's going. "Yeah…"

"Like how he likes to hide things in plain sight?"

I don't like where this is going at all. "Okay…"

"You know that big black granite thing in the family room?"

I flash back to me, lounging in front of the TV, feet propped up on the big black granite thing in the family room. I remember one time I accidentally knocked a mug of tea all over it, and there was that other time I was doing an art project and hammering pieces of plywood on top of it.

Eyes popping out of their sockets, I turn to Uncle Tom. **"I'VE BEEN USING A NUCLEAR BOMB AS A COFFEE TABLE?"**

He smirks. "Last place you'd ever look, right?"

"But…I…" About a million words try to careen out of my lips, but they crash into each other, clogging my throat with wreckage. "What if I had accidentally set it off?"

Uncle Tom dismisses my freak-out with a wave. "Oh, don't worry. There's no way. That container is made of boron carbide. Bombproof, bulletproof, fireproof. The only way to open it is with the three keys."

I rub my throbbing temples. "Keys? What keys?"

"We built it so that each of The Families would have one key, and it only opens if you have all three. That was my idea. I figured, if the bomb can only be used if everyone agrees to it, that would prevent us from turning it on each other."

I raise an eyebrow. "That worked out great."

Major Morton crosses his muscular arms. "We're all just wasting time standing here. Why don't we organize a rescue mission to get Manson back?"

"You don't think they'll see that coming?" Tom's head whips toward him. "They'll kill him immediately if we do that."

Major Morton glares at him. "So what's your idea?"

"We have to negotiate. We'll only get him back with their cooperation."

Major Morton shoots him a condescending look. "Negotiate with what? They're holding all the cards! I don't think pretty-pleases are going to do it, Tom."

"Didn't we capture a bunch of their soldiers this morning?"

"They were rescued in the raid that took Manson. We've got no leverage." He pauses, pensive, scratching the sandpaper-like stubble under his chin. "Can we offer them a ransom?"

Uncle Tom shakes his head. "Jade's got more money than we'll ever have in our lifetimes."

"Then we have to go in after him. I don't see a lot of other options."

The two of them stare, deadlocked, flinging daggers at each other with their eyes. And then they turn to me. "So, what do we do, Fiona?"

My head snaps up. "Me? Why are you asking me?"

Uncle Tom struggles for a second, like he can't quite get the words out. "Well, your dad and I talked about this possibility as tensions were starting to escalate." His hand squeezes my shoulder, and I know I'm not going to like what comes next. "And he told me that if anything were to happen to him…that you should take over."

"What? No." I wave my arms in front of me, trying to ward the crazy away. "Are you insane? I can't run this place!"

"You have to."

"I am thirteen, Uncle Tom! Thirteen! Do I look like an evil genius to you?"

"Those were his wishes. Are." Uncle Tom corrects himself. "Sorry. Those are his wishes."

"No! You do it! You're his second in command! You actually know what's going on around here!"

Major Morton pipes up. "I'm kind of with Fiona on this one, Tom. This just sounds like a bad idea, and she clearly doesn't want to."

"Look," Uncle Tom puts up his hands. "Guys, I know it sounds crazy. But it's in his will. He was adamant that Fiona take over. He said something like 'blood is everything.'"

"Will?" I blink. Just hearing the word sinks my heart into my stomach. "What are you talking about? Dad's not..." I can't even choke the d-word out. "He's coming back."

"We don't know that," Uncle Tom shakes his head solemnly. "We have to assume he's...dead."

Stunned silence settles onto us like radioactive dust.

And then Uncle Tom stares directly into my eyes and says the words I've been dreading my entire life.

"Fiona, as long as he's gone, you're in charge."

"**Dad,** this is stupid," I said, crossing my arms.

Dad ignored me and continued dragging a wooden training dummy into place. We were in our state-of-the-art training facility, and I had just spent the last half hour helping Dad unpack these practice dummies. He still hadn't told me why I needed to spend my Saturday doing this, but by now I was one-hundred percent sure that, whatever the reason was, it was going to be dumb.

And as usual, I was right.

"Okay, Fiona." Dad finally turned to me, looking more than a little winded. "Now, pay attention, because this might be important one day. I'm going to teach you what to do if you're ever attacked by evil henchmen."

I crossed my arms. "Evil henchmen? You mean like our evil henchmen?"

"No, of course not. Other evil henchmen. Or maybe good guys. You never know in this business. It's an occupational hazard of being a super-villain."

I pinched the bridge of my nose as the headache started to form. Oh, God. Not this again. I wasn't in the mood to have this argument. Plus, I needed to study for a math test.

"Okay, now," Dad continued, oblivious as usual. "Say there are four attackers surrounding you, like this." He gestured at the circle of dummies around him. "What do you do?"

"I run away because I'm clearly outnumbered?"

"Wrong!" Dad stabbed a finger in the air. "In this situation, you do what's known as a Flying-Tornado-Double-Jump-Kick."

"A Flying-Tornado-what?"

"A Flying-Tornado-Double-Jump-Kick is a move, invented by none other than yours truly, that allows you to strike four attackers at the same time."

Ugh. I knew this was going to be a waste of time. Why, oh why, had I let Dad drag me down here?

"You don't believe me?"

"Not at all," I said, shaking my head for emphasis. "This sounds like something you saw in a Jackie Chan movie."

"Actually," Dad said. "Jackie learned it from me."

A snort of derision came out of me. I believed that about as much as I'd believed him when he'd told me he was the one who'd invented duck-billed platypuses.

"You can laugh if you want, but when you see the Flying-Tornado-Double-Jump-Kick in action, you're going to say, and I quote, 'Wow, Dad. That was awesome!' Mark my words, that's what you're going to say."

"Okay, Dad." I shrugged. Sure, I'll say that. Right after squirrels come flying out of my butt.

"Now, pay attention!" Dad assumed a weird kung fu stance in the middle of the training dummies. "To start, you want your feet shoulder-width apart and knees slightly bent, like this—"

"Uh-huh." I settled into the stance.

"—and the trick to the Flying-Tornado-Double-Jump-Kick is that you need to know where all four attackers are at all times. The moment you strike, all four limbs become deadly weapons, and you want to be sure they all connect with their targets—"

"All right."

"—and most important of all, you need the element of surprise on your side. You don't want your attackers to know you're about to do this insanely awesome move. So what you want to do is act all scared." He held out his hands in front of him and pretended to tremble in fear. "And then, when they least expect it... **HIIII-YAAAA!**"

Dad launched himself into the air, arms and legs flailing in directions I hadn't known arms and legs could flail. It was one of the weirdest, most awkward-looking things I'd ever seen. And to my complete surprise, he actually started to knock one of the dummies over.

But then he twisted his ankle on the landing and bounced off another dummy. Hopping on one foot, he toppled into the remaining targets, taking them both down with all the grace of a bowling ball. He collapsed into a painful-looking heap on the floor, from which twisted limbs—some wooden, some not—jutted out.

As I stood there, the last upright dummy wobbled once, twice, and finally fell over. It took every ounce of strength I had to keep a straight face as I said, "Wow Dad. That was… awesome."

It feels like only yesterday that Dad was trying to teach me the Flying-Tornado-Double-Jump-Kick. I remember a lot of stuff about that day. Mostly how hard I laughed and how long it took me to catch my breath. How could I possibly have taken that lesson seriously?

Me. A super-villain. Yeah, right. Like that day would ever come.

But now, that day had come. I would give anything to turn back the clock. Maybe then I could pay more attention to what he was trying to teach me.

I don't know how to do a Flying-Tornado-Double-Jump-Kick. In fact, I have no idea how to defend myself at all. Some super-villain I'm turning out to be.

However, then something Dad said echoes in my brain.

I just wanted to make sure…that in case anything should happen…you can protect yourself.

I look down at my black metallic arm. Is this situation what he meant? Did Dad somehow…know this would happen?

A training dummy stands guard like a silent sentry in front of me.

I scowl at it, placing all my worries and fears on those broad wooden shoulders. It stares back, all calm and serene, its hollow eye-sockets wondering why there are sparks coming out of my head.

You want to see sparks? I'll show you sparks…

I flick open the lighter, bring the flame up to my wrist, and work the color-coded buttons.

I'm not useless or helpless. To anyone who thinks I am, this is what's going to happen to them.

I raise my arm and open my palm. Instead of the jet of fire I expect, a giant, rolling fireball shoots out. I scream and jump back. The fireball whizzes past the mannequin, travelling in a lazy downward arc before slamming into the concrete floor and exploding into an inferno.

Whoa! What the…?

I look down at my wrist. I meant to push the yellow button, but instead, the orange one is depressed. I pushed the wrong button.

I look up at the blazing lake of fire I just created. As the flames scorch the concrete and start to die out, all I can think is, Oh man, I have **GOT** to do that again.

I lock my eyes on a spot a far away, in the opposite corner of the training facility, and form my metallic right hand into a claw. A miniature flame ignites with a gentle fwoomf, but I keep my hand half-closed, containing the fire.

Still focusing on that spot, I bring my arm back, raise my left leg, and I hurl the fire like I'm pitching the most important fastball in game seven of the World Series.

The fireball flies way further than I thought it would. It soars across the training room, slamming into an un-opened crate and blowing it apart with the force of a rocket-propelled grenade. Burning dummy parts catapult into the air, showering the area with charred limbs.

I look down at my metallic arm. Fireballs? I can throw fireballs? Holy crap, little flamethrower. Where have you been all my life?

An electronic ringing cuts through the smoky air, jarring me back to reality.

I shut off the flamethrower, making sure the blue flame flowing through the clear tubes goes out before I reach for my cell phone. I turn it over in my metallic hand, squinting at the screen.

It's Jai.

"Hey," he says.

"Hey." I smile. After everything that has happened, I so need someone to talk to right now.

"So...is it true?"

"Is what true?"

"The news about your dad. That Jade's got him."

I sigh. Guess news like this travels pretty fast. "Yeah. It is."

"Wow." A pause. "How are you holding up?"

"Not good. It feels like my head's about to..." a flaming wooden head rolls by "...explode."

"Maybe I can help."

"Help me explode?"

"No, help with your dad."

I shake my head emphatically. "Jai, no."

"I could ask my dad to... I don't know, maybe see if he can talk Jade out of it?" His voice sounds all echo-y on the other end. Maybe he's in a hallway or something?

"Your dad?" I scoff. "He's even more unpredictable than Jade is. Remember last year when he blew up Mount Tantalus?"

"Yeah, I guess..."

I step over a charred torso. "Why did he do that again? Why was he so mad at that poor mountain?"

Jai coughs. "I think he said it was blocking his view."

"Right. Yeah, I don't think he would help this situation very much." I kick an arm out of the way.

"Well, maybe I could—"

"Jai, don't get involved. Please. The situation's dangerous enough as it is. I don't want to put you in danger, too."

There's a long pause, but he knows I'm not budging. He wouldn't want to put me in danger, either. "Are you sure you can handle this?"

"Yeah," I reassure him. "I have to."

Are you sure you can handle this? Jai's voice echoes in my head long after he hangs up. It's the question I've been asking myself ever since I came down here. Only problem is, what I told him was a lie. I can't handle this. I can't even begin to handle this.

Let's get realistic. A thirteen-year-old girl in charge of an evil empire? There's no word in the dictionary for how completely doomed I am right now. To top it all off, Dad's life is hanging in the balance. If I make a mistake, I may never see Dad again, ever. It would be completely, one-hundred-percent my fault.

I stop because I've walked into a ring of practice dummies. Four of them surround me, and I hear Dad's words.

So say there are four attackers surrounding you, like this. What do you do?

I click the yellow button on my wrist. Well, Dad, I may not know how to do a Flying-Tornado-Double-Jump-Kick, but I can do this...

I spin, sending staccato bursts of flame in every direction, until all four mannequins are on fire. One of them collapses, its flaming head detaching on impact and rolling off into a nearby corner. Somehow, that makes me feel better.

"You're getting pretty good with that thing." Uncle Tom's voice cuts through my thoughts.

"Remind me not to get on your bad side," Major Morton adds.

I try to smile but I can't. I know they don't come bearing gifts.

"I'll try to take care of as many of the logistics and repair issues as possible, but you're going to have to decide how we proceed. And we only have—" Uncle Tom looks down at his gold watch "—twenty-two hours left to make that decision."

I massage the back of my neck, begging the throbbing headache to go away, but it refuses. It just keeps building and building, until finally I can't take it anymore.

"Why would he do this to me, Uncle Tom?" I ask, exasperated. "Every single time Dad and I have talked about this, I've told him that I don't want to be a super-villain!"

He shakes his head. "I don't know, Fiona. Maybe he figured if you tried it, you'd like it."

"Great." I shake my head in disbelief. "Do I look happy right now? All this just makes me want to get into a helicopter and fly as far away from here as possible."

"I know, I know." Uncle Tom nods and squeezes my shoulder. "I don't like it any more than you do, but someone's going to have to make a call. Right now, that someone is you."

I try to speak, but nothing comes out.

The panic is back again, like a net that keeps getting thrown over me every time I have to make a decision. Every strand is a what if and every knot is a what if I don't. Together they entangle and trap me; I can't get away.

What am I supposed to say? What if I say the wrong thing?

Major Morton cuts in, seeming to sense my paralysis. "Should I begin drawing up plans for the rescue mission?"

I stay silent.

"Fiona, listen to me." Uncle Tom takes a step forward. "We have to negotiate."

"With what?" Major Morton turns to him. "We have nothing they want."

"It's better than a suicidal attack that gets everyone killed!"

There's a long pause as they stare at each other like two bulls with their horns locked.

I turn away and stare at the burned mannequins. Charred practice dummies surround me, and I can almost feel the gazes from their empty eye sockets and burnt-out skulls boring into me, watching, waiting, and judging.

I'm back in those smoke-filled corridors, and every path is so terrible I don't want to go down any of them.

"What do you want us to do, Fiona?" Uncle Tom asks again.

I'm not sure if I'm imagining it or if it's some strange coincidence, but all the featureless wooden heads of the mannequins are swiveled in my direction. They wait for my answer, hang on my every word.

Uncle Tom's right about the rescue mission. They'd see us coming a mile away. Heck, I'd see us coming a mile away, and I don't have the slightest idea what I'm doing. We don't even know where Dad is being held, so we'd have to search every room in the air base until we found him. There's no way we'd get to him in time.

However, we can't negotiate either. As Major Morton said, we have nothing they want.

So is that it? Are there no other options? Are we stuck between a rock and a horrible place?

Come on. Think. There's got to be another way. There's always another way.

There is a third choice. There's always been a third choice, but it's so unspeakable nobody even considered it. It's so clearly wrong, it's never been an option.

I turn around. They're both standing there, staring at me with expectant eyes. They're not going to like what I'm about to say.

"Well?"

I swallow hard and then force myself to say it.

"We have to give them the bomb."

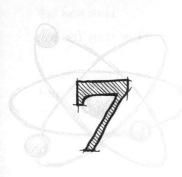

As soon as the words leave my mouth, I can see they hate the idea. The thing that catches me off-guard is how much they hate it.

"Absolutely not," says Uncle Tom.

"Are you insane?" asks Jim.

"That's the most—"

"Completely irresponsible—"

"Guys, guys, guys," I say, my voice barely audible in all the shouting. "We have to do this. It's the only way to get Dad back."

"Yes, but this is a nuclear bomb we're talking about, Fiona," Uncle Tom says, clenching his fists. "We can't let it fall into the wrong hands."

"But they can't set it off," I say.

He looks at me. Even though his brow is furrowed, his silence lets me know I'm onto something.

"They need all three keys to use it," I continue. "Jade only has one. And that case is bombproof, bulletproof, and fireproof, right? Those were your words."

"That's true."

"So, it doesn't matter if we hand it over to them. They can't set it off."

Another tense few seconds of silence settle on us as Uncle Tom mulls it over. Finally, it's Major Morton who speaks up. "She does have a point, Tom."

Uncle Tom shakes his head. "Try to understand, Fiona. It's not just about the bomb. If we cave to their demands, even once, that will send the signal that we're weak."

"So what? Why do I care what they think?"

"If they think we're weak, they'll hit us again. And then we'll be right back in this situation, arguing about some other crisis. I guarantee it. Only next time, they'll have a nuclear weapon, and we won't have anything else to bargain with."

I try to counter that, but I can't. I know he's right.

For some reason, my thoughts drift to Jai, and how much he likes scaring all the other students. I always thought it was an ego thing, but now I realize that instilling fear in people has its perks. Nobody messes with you if they're scared.

"If Manson were here, I'm sure he'd—"

"Dad's not here, Uncle Tom. I'm all you have left."

The headache returns. To be accurate, it never left, but it's getting worse. I wince. The day keeps going and going and seems like it will never end. I wouldn't be surprised if I wake up tomorrow to find I've aged a decade.

"I wish Dad were here right now, too. He'd come up with some genius solution. One that doesn't involve giving them what they want, and that doesn't involve a suicidal rescue mission. He'd figure out some way to pull it off without firing a shot, and Jade would never know what happened until it's over."

Tom nods. It's the one thing we've agreed on today. "I bet it'd involve lasers or satellites or something."

"And robots." Major Morton chimes in.

I nod, smirking. "It would definitely involve robots."

If there's ever the slightest way to work robots into a situation, Dad will figure out how to do it. One time he got a parking ticket from some traffic cop who clearly didn't know who he was dealing with. Dad spent an entire month designing a robot disguised as a donut so he could sneak it into the police station. Once nobody was looking, the "donut" scurried over to a computer and plugged itself in, allowing Dad to hack into the system and erase the parking ticket from existence. Spending thousands of dollars to build a robot for the sole purpose of erasing a fifty-dollar ticket didn't make much sense to me, but that's the thing with Dad. If he can come up with a clever way to get out of a situation, he'll do it even if it doesn't make sense.

"So let's get him back," I say with as much authority as a five-foot-tall acting super-villain can muster. "Once he's back, he can come up with some genius idea to retrieve the NOVA."

Once we get Dad back, I can go back to worrying about math tests, and Dad can go back to being the super-villain in charge.

Major Morton nods. "All right, we have our orders. I'll have my men pack up the NOVA." He heads toward the exit.

"I know, Uncle Tom. I know. You hate this plan."

"I do."

"I'm just doing the best I can. All the other options will get Dad killed. And I'm not going to be the one that lets that happen."

Uncle Tom relents a little at that. "I know." Finally, he turns and walks to the exit. "I just hope you don't end up being the one that gets us all killed."

The door slams behind him and I'm alone.

A whole swarm of butterflies suddenly hatches in my stomach, and I have to grab something to keep from falling over. I feel like throwing up. As the world spins around me, I keep replaying Uncle Tom's words in my head. Why did he have to say that? Doesn't he know how hard this is for me already? And most importantly, what if he's right? What if I am about to get us all killed?

I hate being a super-villain.

The sun sets as we arrive, lighting up the sky with splashes of orange and red. It would be breathtaking if it weren't so ominous.

"We're approaching the landing zone," Pilot Mike informs us over our headsets. Major Morton gives him the thumbs-up, and our helicopter begins its descent.

An old abandoned factory. Why do hostage exchanges always happen in creepy abandoned places? Sometimes we super-villains can be shockingly uncreative.

Oh God. I just thought "we super-villains," didn't I?

"You don't have to come in with us." Major Morton's gruff voice sounds tiny and distant over the headsets.

"I told you, I'm coming. I'm not going to send you into danger and wait in the helicopter for you to get back."

"You're thirteen. It's my job to protect you."

"And you did that in the tunnels. Maybe I'll be able to return the favor this time."

Major Morton turns and gives me a pat on the shoulder. His hand is so huge he could pick me up by my head if he wanted to. "You know, one day, when you grow up, you might turn out to be a pretty good evil genius yourself."

If I heard those words in another situation, I would roll my eyes and tell him to stop being stupid. But today, a smile breaks through. "Thanks, Major Morton."

"Call me Jim."

We land in the parking lot in front of the building, and one by one our soldiers disembark, their rifles up and ready. After a tense moment of scanning for targets, they declare the parking lot secure and return to the helicopter. Grunting, they unload the NOVA onto a heavy-duty construction dolly, and it still takes all six of them. I can only guess how many hundreds of pounds that thing weighs.

Smashed windows line the walls of the factory, and the crumbling bricks make it look like it barely survived a war. If someone searched for the word foreboding online, this building would be on the first page. I shudder as we approach it and wonder whether staying on the helicopter may not have been a bad idea after all. Then I remember I'm doing this for Dad. We'll just get in and get out as fast as possible.

The front door creaks as Jim opens it. He enters first, followed by the soldiers pushing the NOVA, and me, close behind.

Piles of old crates tower over us, and industrial machines lie broken and covered with dust. The only light source in the entire room is the sliver of sunlight filtering through one of the broken windows. Above us, a network of rickety-looking metal catwalks crisscrosses in every direction. All of this adds up to creepiness that coats everything along with that dust.

We stop when we reach the center of the factory floor. There's no one in sight.

A sergeant, the one with the thick New York accent who helped us during the invasion, scans the room. "Is something supposed to happen?" he says.

Jim hisses, "Stay alert, soldier."

"I don't like it. Too many places to hide," another soldier says.

The silence hangs over us like a black cloud. The Storm Troopers survey their surroundings, pointing their guns at the smallest sounds. I hold my breath and wait for something to happen. It's so quiet I can almost hear the hairs on the back of my neck stand on end.

My phone rings. The noise pierces the air like a bullet, and everyone jumps. Who the heck is calling me now? If this is a telemarketer I'm going to personally have their office carpet-bombed.

I fumble around for my phone. When I finally manage to wrestle it out of my pocket, I hold it up in the dim light and read the number on the screen. Restricted.

I answer. "He-hello?"

The voice that responds sounds computer synthesized, like in movies where the kidnapper tries to hide their identity. "We weren't expecting you to be here."

I gesture at Jim, pointing frantically at my headset.

Is it them? he mouths.

I nod.

"W-where's my dad?"

"Did you bring the NOVA?"

Jim gestures to the men, pointing at his earpiece and then holding up two fingers. Channel two. One by one, they adjust their radios to tune into my frequency.

"Yes. It's right here," I say.

"Place it on the ground."

I look over at Jim, and he nods back. The six soldiers gather around the bomb and carefully hoist it off the dolly. It makes a loud thud when it touches the floor.

"All right, you've got your bomb. Now give me my dad back."

"Your father will be delivered once we check that this really is what you say it is."

"Fine. Go ahead and check it."

"We will. In our lab," the robotic voice says. "You and your men may leave now."

"What?" I shout back. "No! That wasn't the deal. The deal was, we give you the NOVA, and you give back my dad."

"No," the voice says, betraying no emotion. "The deal was you give us the NOVA, and we don't kill your dad. We promised nothing about returning him."

My plan falls like a house of cards. I want to whip the phone at the ground.

"That," I seethe through gritted teeth "is a crappy, crappy deal and you know it. I'm taking the NOVA back unless you give me my dad."

"That would be a very bad idea. Right now, there are about a hundred guns pointed at you and your men. If you attempt to take the NOVA, we will shoot to kill."

Jim and his soldiers take cover, ducking nimbly behind crates, machinery, anything they can find. They point their rifles up, scanning for targets, but they find none in the murky blackness.

"Get down," Jim hisses from behind a pillar. That's when I realize I'm still standing out in the open, completely exposed.

The computerized voice hisses in my ear. "Last chance for you and your men to leave alive."

I scan the warehouse, but I don't see anyone. Maybe they're bluffing. Struggling to keep the fear out of my voice, I say, "I'm not leaving without my dad."

The person on the other end of the line is silent for a moment. Then finally he says, "Suit yourself."

A bullet brushes past my fingertips, slams into my phone, and shatters it. I fall backward, wheezing, as I collapse onto the cold, hard concrete. If my head had been one-eighth of an inch to the left, I'd be dead.

Around me, bullets fly from every direction as my men return fire.

It's all I can do to curl into a ball and try not to get hit. I should be screaming, but I don't. It all seems so surreal.

Someone grabs my wrist. It's Jim. He drags me out of the open and behind a nearby machine. "Are you injured?"

I blink, uncomprehending. He shakes me again, accidentally banging my head against the metal. "Are you injured?"

Finally, I shake my head no.

Jim nods, squeezing my shoulder before running off to join the other soldiers, firing hot death back at our attackers. Shakily, I look down at my left hand, the one that I had been holding over my ear as Jim dragged me to safety. It's trembling so hard I can barely control it. And there's blood on my fingers.

Around me, my men unleash a fresh volley of bullets into the darkness surrounding us, but Jade's men aren't charging at us like video-game characters. They're hidden in the walkways and abandoned machines.

"Exit?" Jim screams at his squad.

"Fire exit," the New York sergeant shouts back, between volleys. "That way."

"Let's go!"

The squad runs toward a corner of the factory, weaving in and out of the winding corridors, and I stay as close to Jim as I can. Bullets fly at us, and sparks shower us from where they impact the metal machinery. It's dark now, the sun having set, and all I can see are muzzle flashes.

"Locked," the sergeant shouts, pointing at the handle. It's wrapped up in a great steel chain, and a giant padlock hangs from it. I curse under my breath.

Jim seems unfazed. "Blow it open, Bill."

"Yes, sir!"

Bill drops to a knee and starts wiring the doorframe with explosives. Meanwhile, gunfire continues to rain down around us. Jim signals to me, palm down, waving toward the floor. I hit the ground as the other soldiers move into defensive positions around the door, firing into the inky blackness.

Bill inserts wire into a putty-like explosive. He's working as fast as he can, but a part of me wants to jump on his back and shout at him to go faster. Every cell in my body wants me to get out, yet we're stuck, waiting for him to finish. Between bursts of gunfire, I see the dark outlines of enemy soldiers closing in on our position. As long as the door's still closed, we're trapped, and they know it.

A bullet flies past, and Bill yelps and crumples to the floor. My hand flies to my mouth as Jim rushes to his side. He's screaming something, but I can't hear what.

We're doomed. We are so doomed. The door is locked, we're trapped in a corner, and soldiers are closing in. The Storm Troopers blast at the shadows closing in, but I know it's not enough. There are only eight of us, and who knows how many of them.

My lighter is in my hand. I've been flicking the wheel without even realizing it. This is it. It's now or never. My flamethrower lights up, and I work the controls. I've just decided I don't want to hide anymore. If I'm going to die, I want to go down fighting.

Jim sees me standing up, and his eye goes wide. "Fiona, get down. What are you doing?"

Ignoring him, I step into the open. I whip a fireball at a group of approaching silhouettes. It explodes, sending them running every which way. I don't have time to dwell on their fate, as a muzzle flash catches my eye and a burst of automatic fire whizzes past my head. I zero in on the raised metal walkway it came from and throw another fireball. It explodes, collapsing the entire structure. Then, I throw one into the ceiling. Debris rains down, and the twisted metal slams into a crane, causing it to topple over, blocking one of the paths the attackers were using to charge at us.

The Storm Troopers stare. Jim stares. Even injured Bill stares.

Jim is the first one to come to his senses. "Keep shooting! Keep shooting!"

The remaining Storm Troopers, freed from having to cover the blocked path, re-form around the remaining corridor. They reload, and fire at anything that moves.

I look over to see Jim finish wiring the explosives on the door. He flicks a lighter, a dented Zippo, and lights the fuse. "Fire in the hole!"

Everyone takes cover. I dive behind a wooden box and cover my ears. The shock wave reverberates in my chest, my teeth, and my skull. If I weren't covering my ears, my eardrums would have blown apart. But when I look up, relief floods over me. The door is gone.

I sprint through the door, and the first breath of cold night air is the sweetest thing I've ever tasted. Above me, our helicopter is still circling, a buzzing beacon of light searching for us. "Over here!" I shout, waving at it until my hands are a blur of motion above me.

Behind me, Jim and another Storm Trooper carry Bill out. Even as they do, he keeps firing his weapon at our attackers.

Our helicopter lands in the field in front of us. I can see Pilot Mike through the windows, gesturing wildly.

Something slams into my wrist with a clang, and I wince as my arm whips violently around my body from the impact. It takes a few seconds of confused blinking for me to realize there's now a bullet-sized dent on my metallic wrist. I've just been shot. And I don't like it one bit.

The enemy pours out of the metal doorway after us. Amidst the barrage of gunfire and heavy smoke, they're still charging.

I turn, narrowing my eyes. All right, buddies. You want me so bad? Well, come and get me.

I bring my arm back, take aim, and then I throw the largest fireball I've thrown yet. It hits the building right on target, right above the doorframe. The resulting explosion collapses the front wall, destroying the exit and filling it with rubble. I wait a few seconds, surveying my smoking handiwork. The exit's closed. They can't follow us anymore.

"Fiona! Come on!" Jim's call blares through my headset.

The others are already on the helicopter, waving at me to run.

I take one last look at the smoldering rubble before joining them. Jim hoists me into the chopper, and then, surrounded by my Storm Troopers, I lift off and head for home.

The second our skids touch the ground, the medics slide the door open and attach electrodes and monitors to Bill before hoisting him onto a stretcher.

"Hey Major," he says. "I forget, if I see a light, am I supposed to go toward it or away from it?"

That gets a chuckle out of Jim. "Make sure you give him an extra shot of morphine," he tells one of the medics.

Bill hoots as they carry him away. "Best day ever!"

Leave it to a Storm Trooper to make jokes even when he's been shot. However, jokes and laughter only exist as brief distractions from reality, and when I look up, I see reality marching over to us.

And reality looks mad.

"What happened out there?" Uncle Tom shouts over the sound of the chopper's slowing rotors.

"We got ambushed is what happened," Jim says.

"I know that. Did we get Manson out?"

Jim flexes his jaw, but doesn't say anything.

"What about the NOVA?"

More silence.

"God...damn it!" Uncle Tom throws his headset to the ground, smashing the expensive-looking thing into a million shards of plastic. "This was a setup from the beginning. Was he even in the building?"

"No, he wasn't." Jim glares at him, slinging his still-smoking rifle over his shoulder. "But what was in the building was an entire army your intel couldn't see."

Uncle Tom narrows his eyes. "What are you saying, Major?"

"I'm saying…" Jim takes a step forward, jamming a gloved finger into Uncle Tom's chest. "That you sent six men into an ambush with a hundred guns pointed at them! You almost got us all killed."

Uncle Tom smacks Jim's hand away and jabs his own finger into Jim's chest. "There was no way to know how many of Jade's men were in that building! We only learned the drop-off point an hour before the deadline."

"Maybe you can negotiate that out of them next time." Jim says, spitting that word out like it's made of poison and swatting Uncle Tom's finger away. He doesn't even try to hide the disgust on his face. "Let me know how your next round of negotiations goes."

Not even the helicopter rotors can drown out their shouting.

"You still think we should have gone in guns blazing? That would have gotten everyone killed."

"What we just did almost got everyone killed!"

"Now we have no NOVA and no Manson!"

"And whose fault is that, Tom?"

"Okay, stop!" To everyone's surprise, the voice is mine. They turn, gaping at my outburst. "It was my fault." I stare down at my hand. My palm is still smeared with blood, but I try not to think about it as I wipe it on my pleated skirt. "It was my decision to give them the NOVA. I'm the one that almost got everyone killed."

The awkward silence settles on us like an uncomfortable fog. I want someone to break it, but none of us do.

"Sir? Sir?" A technician wearing a black and red jumpsuit runs into the hangar, out of breath, clutching a piece of paper. "This just…this just came in…" he says, not sure who to give it to.

Uncle Tom snatches it out of his hand and reads it out loud. "Give us the key in 24 hours or we kill Manson—"

A volcano erupts inside me, and I storm up to Tom, grab the paper, and tear it to pieces. Then I tear the pieces to shreds. And then I light my flamethrower and burn the shreds to a crisp.

When there's nothing left, I collapse, sobbing, as I sink onto the concrete.

How could I be so naïve and stupid? Super-villains don't keep their word. Double-crossing is the first thing super-villains do. That's Super-Villainy 101.

"So I take it we're done with negotiations, then?" Jim peers at me with his one good eye, then Uncle Tom.

None of us answer. None of us need to.

"All right." Jim nods. "I'll draw up plans for an all-out invasion of Jade's base."

Tom pipes up. "Major, are we certain this is what we want to do?"

Jim shakes his head. "There are no other options, Tom. Not anymore."

And without another word, Jim turns and heads toward the hangar door, his heavy boots thumping on the concrete. When I look at Uncle Tom, there's no reassurance in his eyes that everything will be okay. Nothing that says we can go back to being a normal super-villainous family and I can forget any of this ever happened. His cloudy blue eyes are as hopeless as mine.

I'm in my room, curled up in bed with a wad of bandages around my ear. After fussing over me for what seemed like hours, Uncle Tom finally left me alone. I could have spent the whole day in the hangar, but I got sick of the technicians and mechanics staring at the tears running down my face. If only they could fix it. If only they could tighten a bolt or fill up a gas tank to make all my problems disappear.

I'm not meant for a normal life. As much I want to believe it, I'm not normal. Normal gets stuffed in a locker, as Jai would say, but right now I'd give anything to be stuffed in a locker.

"**Did** I ever tell you the story of the Scorpion and the Frog?"

I looked up from my homework, annoyed at the distraction. "No, Dad, but I'm sure you're about to tell me."

Dad pulled up a chair, going into full-on storyteller mode. I hate it when he does that. So melodramatic.

"So there's this river, and a scorpion that wants to get across. He asks a nearby frog to take him, and the frog tells him no. When asked why, the frog says he's afraid of being stung, but the scorpion answers that he shouldn't worry, because if he stings the frog, they'll both drown."

"Dad, is this going to be a long story? Because it's a school night—"

Dad ignored me. "So the frog starts swimming and swimming with that scorpion on his back. But halfway across the river, the scorpion does, in fact, sting the frog, dooming them both. And as they sink, the frog asks the scorpion, 'Why did you sting me? Now we're both going to die.' And the scorpion replies, 'It's in my nature.'"

"Why are you telling me this, Dad? Am I the frog, and I'm supposed to be careful of who to trust?"

"The frog? No!" Dad looked me right in the eye, placing both his hands on my tiny shoulders. "Fiona, you're the scorpion."

All that time spent pretending. All those years wasted, trying to be normal. What a colossal waste of time and effort. At least Jai understood. Ruby, too. They never pretended. They never hid their true nature. I'm the only one who tried.

My room is a perfect example. It's boring and normal-looking, but the normalcy isn't by accident. I painted the normal on, and it's as heavy as lead. But it's also as fake as smoke. Peel back the façade and it shows exactly what my real life's like.

A boy-band poster hangs above my bed, but I don't even know who it's of. The other girls at school fawned over them, so I pretended to fawn too. Behind that poster is a hole in the wall, hiding a black getaway bag. Dad helped me fill it with plane tickets, fake passports, and enough money to escape to Tahiti if I need to.

The red bookcase next to my desk, filled with fantasy novels, is a fake too. A secret passage is hidden behind it.

Even my wrought-iron bed isn't ordinary. Dad insists I keep a loaded pistol there, right under my pillow. Even though I hate guns, it sits there every night, poking me in my sleep, reminding me even in my dreams that I'm not now, nor ever will be, normal.

But it doesn't matter anymore. All the stupid things I used to fight with Dad about are shadows in my rear-view mirror. Dad's gone, and Jim's raid will probably fail, and I'll probably never see either one of them again.

All I want in the entire world is to get Dad back home. But I'm not cut out for this. I've only been doing it for a day, and I can feel my hair going grey. I'm not smart or ruthless or…evil. I've already proven myself to be the most useless super-villain in the entire universe. I suck.

The phone by my bed rings. I stare at it, not wanting to pick it up, but finally, after the third ring, I answer.

"Hey," Jai says.

"Hey," I reply, trying to sound normal despite the tears running down my face.

"Is everything all right?"

"Yeah, I'm okay." I walk over to the window and look outside. The world is disturbingly bright and sunny this morning, taunting me with its happiness.

"How come you haven't been picking up your cell?"

Maybe because it's lying in a hundred pieces on a factory floor? That's what I want to say. But instead I say, "I…uh…I lost it."

Silence.

"You don't have to lie. I know what happened."

I'm taken aback, but quickly regain my composure. "What do you mean?"

"You lost the NOVA, didn't you?"

I turn from the window so fast I almost drop the phone. What? How could he possibly know about that so quickly?

Jai somehow responds to the question I didn't ask. "I told you. There's not a lot that goes on around here that we don't know about."

I hesitate for a second. I shouldn't tell him anything. He's not part of the family, he's not one of the Storm Troopers, he's technically a rival, but against my better judgment, I blurt it out. "I don't know what to do, Jai. Jade has the NOVA but she didn't give Dad back. So now she has the bomb and Dad, and there's nothing I can do."

Silence. A long silence. And then finally, "You're going to attack Jade, aren't you?"

My mouth drops open. Trying to think fast, I launch into my well-reasoned explanation as to why his guess is wrong. Unfortunately, all that comes out is "Uh…no…"

"You're a terrible liar, Sparky. I think that's adorable."

I sigh and let myself fall back against the soft cotton sheets on my bed. I really do suck at this.

"Let me help."

That, I'm not expecting. I blink, stunned. "What? Jai, no. We already talked about this. I don't want to put you in danger."

"You already have. You put us all in danger when you handed over the NOVA."

My jaw drops open as I stare at the ceiling. "Wh-what? I did?"

"Think about it. Jade has the bomb and one key. What do you think she's going to try to get next?"

"The other keys."

"And who has the other two keys?"

"Well, me and…" My voice trails off. Now I know what he's getting at, and I don't like it one bit.

"If we don't take Jade out, if we don't get things back to the way they were, she'll eventually come after us. My family's in danger now too."

The magnitude of my actions starts to dawn on me. Uncle Tom was right. Handing over the NOVA was an even more dangerous move than I thought. Rather than fix anything, it made things more complicated, and now Jai's family is getting dragged into it too. And in the middle of it all, a nuclear bomb sits, waiting to wake up and wipe out all of us.

In two days, I've managed to bring all of us to the brink of World War III.

"So, do you agree?" Jai's says, his voice jolting me back to reality.

"Uhhh…" He's been talking, but I haven't been listening. I drag my eyes away from the ceiling and try to focus. "Agree about what?"

Jai sighs. "That your Storm Troopers can't rescue your dad on their own. We've seen them in action. They're good, pretty much unbeatable in a fight, actually. But for a rescue mission, I'm not so sure. Do you even know where your dad's being held?"

"No."

"I do."

My ears perk up.

"And," Jai continues, "I have a way to get in."

I can't believe what I'm hearing. Up until thirty seconds ago, I assumed the rescue mission was a lost cause. I had accepted that I might never see my dad again.

But now? Could we actually pull this off?

"So, what do you say?" Jai asks. "Shall we form an alliance?"

An alliance. I let the strange-sounding word percolate in my brain.

The very idea of an alliance of any kind among The Families should be scoffed at, ridiculed, and dismissed as being as likely as a Mayan apocalypse.

If Dad were here, he'd say it was preposterous.

However, Dad isn't here, and today has already been a day of so many firsts. What's one more?

I roll onto my side and curl my knees into my chest. "What do you have in mind, Jai?"

The rumbling floor shifts underneath me and I stumble, crashing against a metal bulkhead. We're in a tiny room in a tiny sub, five hundred feet beneath the surface of the ocean. Jai's cabin barely holds anything—just a bed and a table— and I've crashed into both a dozen times already. Submarines may be a lot of things, but they definitely aren't built for the uncoordinated.

"Jeez, Jai. I can't believe you actually live in a submarine."

Jai arches an eyebrow. "I thought I told you before."

"Probably. But I always thought you were kidding. I mean, what fourteen-year-old actually has his own submarine?"

Jai grins, pointing two thumbs up at his face. "This guy!"

I laugh. I guess there are still a few things I don't know about Jai. "Well, I love what you've done with the place," I say, surveying the bare walls.

"Hey, shut up." Jai says. "When your room randomly tilts forty-five degrees, stuff doesn't say upright for long."

"Yeah, I guess." I snort. "There are a few downsides of living in a submarine, aren't there?"

"Some. But on the other hand, I can fire torpedoes. Can you fire torpedoes?"

I glare at him. "What would you even fire at, Jai? Another submarine? Literally nobody else has a submarine."

"That's...true..." Jai says.

"Seems kind of ridiculous, if you ask me."

Jai glowers. "Says the girl with a flamethrower strapped to her wrist."

70

I open my mouth for a brilliant comeback, but…nothing. Fine. He wins this round.

"Fifteen minutes to target," a metallic voice announces from the intercom on the wall by the door.

"Okay, thanks," Jai says into the microphone before turning to me. "You ready?"

"I think so. Let's go over the plan one more time."

I turn my attention to the blueprints rolled out over the metal table. Squinting at the maze of diagrams in the buzzing fluorescent light, I'm amazed by the detail. I can see how many potted plants there are, which way a door swings, where all the cameras are, where the blind spots are. The amount of detail is staggering.

"How were you able to get all this information?"

"Let's just say Jade has a blind spot."

"Which is?"

Jai smirks at me. "The water."

All of a sudden all the weird underwater equipment Dad installed a few summers ago makes sense. After all, we live on an island, and I remember asking him what all that stuff did. Back then, he said it was to keep dolphins away, and I just chalked it up to his craziness. But over the past few days, I've started to understand that Dad isn't so crazy. Quite the opposite. He was never looking for dolphins. He was looking for spies.

"You've been spying on them?"

"Not me. My dad."

Oh. Right. Him.

I've often said that my dad's crazy, but when you get right down to it, eccentric is a better word. When it comes to pure, all-out crazy, my dad can't even hold a candle to The Captain. He's not even in the same universe. I heard that The Captain ordered his men to shoot birds near his ship on sight, because he thought they were drone-birds sent by the government.

"How long has this been going on?"

"Long enough." Jai shrugs. "We know where all their storm drains go, where their pipes lead, where they keep their planes, where they keep the fuel for their planes. Our spies probably know their base better than they do." Jai smirks, his strange blue eyes twinkling in the fluorescent light. "Impressed?"

"Impressed…terrified. Somewhere in between those two." As I stare at the amazing amount of detail spread in front of us, all I can think is, if he knows so much about them, how much does he know about us?

Jai shuffles through the pile of maps and takes one out, spreading it on top of the others. This one seems to be some kind of naval map, and all the squiggles and depth markings look like gibberish to me. "Okay, so the sub will take us up to here." He points to an ink blob on the paper, but I have no idea what I'm looking at, so I nod along, pretending to understand. "There's an entrance here to a massive underwater cave network that runs underneath Jade's base."

"Caves? I didn't know there were caves here."

"Nobody did. They're not on any map anywhere. Until we found them." He yanks another map from the stack and spreads it out. This one shows an underground cave system, and the markings make it look like a giant snake, slithering its way through the rock underneath Jade's air base. At least this one I can understand. "We swim out and enter the cave network here." He points at a place on the map marked with a blue dot.

"What do all those red dots mean?" I point to the strange markings with my metallic hand.

"Those are entrances to the base."

"Wait." I squint at the dots. "If Jade doesn't know about these caves, why would she build entrances to her base in them?"

"She didn't," Jai says. "We did."

"What?" I look up, startled. "When did you do that?"

"These were made years ago, way before any of this crazy stuff started to happen. You know, just in case."

"Just in case of what?"

"In case crazy stuff started to happen. Like now. We'd need a way into her base without anyone knowing."

I gape at him. "How did you know any of this would happen?"

"We didn't. We just figured, well…" The twinkle in his eye is back. "You never know when a back door might come in handy."

Now I'm really worried. Don't get me wrong, I'm glad we have a way in and all, but all these revelations make the little paranoid voice in the back of my head go into overdrive. If they punched all these secret back doors into Jade's base without anyone knowing, who's to say they haven't done the same to us?

"So, anyway, from there…" Jai pulls out another map, oblivious to the worry lines spreading across my face, "we'll emerge in this pump station over here, only a few meters away from their high-security vault. That's where they're keeping your dad. Sound good?"

I nod and bite my lip. This plan is getting way too complicated.

Jai turns to me. "You sure you can get that vault open?"

I nod again, but this time I'm confident. "Just get us into the base. I'll take care of the vault."

I unclip my black waterproof bag and rustle through it, making sure I have everything. Tube of lipstick-slash-laser torch, check. Laptop, check. Trusty lighter, check. When Dad gave me most of this stuff I remembered asking questions like, "When would I ever need a laser torch?" And now I'm off to rescue him with a bag full of my "useless" birthday presents.

Jai checks his own gear, gathering stuff he needs from around his cabin. Too bad his stuff is horribly boring. A flashlight. A pair of black gloves. A pair of needle-nose pliers. Yawn.

"Do you have a radio?"

"I don't need a radio," I reply. "I have my cell…" And then I trail off. Oh, right.

"Hmm. Well, I guess we'll have to use mine then…" Jai starts rummaging, looking for it. "And don't worry. When this is all over, I'll get you a new phone for your birthday. A bullet-proof one."

I laugh at that. Right. A bullet-proof cell phone. Where would you even find something like that? Evil Gadgets-R-Us?

"Hey Jai?"

"Hmm?"

"Did you know that our parents used to…you know…not hate each other?"

He slides open a compartment, revealing a drawer full of black ski masks. "I've heard some stories."

"You have? What do you know?"

He shrugs. "Bits and pieces. I know they knew each other in college. I think they used to be roommates, or something."

"What?" Roommates? They can't even stand to be on the same continent! "How did they not kill each other?"

"Apparently, they used to be best friends." He smiles, clearly amused by the bug-eyed expression I'm sporting. "Yeah, I know. Hard to imagine, huh?"

I shake my head. "Not hard. Impossible." The Families have been warring archenemies ever since I can remember. The idea that they used to be friends is ludicrous. "What happened after college?"

"Well, my dad joined the Navy and became the youngest captain in naval history."

"Is that why he makes everyone call him The Captain?"

"Right. Dad loves rubbing it in people's faces." He smirks. "Anyway, Manson did something with weapons—"

"He used to work as a weapons researcher. With the Department of Defense."

"Sure." Jai nods. "And Jade went off and became filthy rich somehow."

"I heard she married a billionaire."

"I've heard that story. I've heard that she's a genius at playing the stock market. And I've also heard she got her money by stealing the world's biggest diamond in the world's biggest diamond heist. Who knows what's actually true?"

I shake my head. Knowing what we know about any of our parents, any of those explanations are equally plausible. "Then what happened?"

"Well, after your dad quit working for the Department of Defense, the three of them banded together to build a super-weapon. I guess that's when all this super-villainy stuff started. Your dad and Tom were the brains, Jade was the money, and my dad gave them a floating lab to work in so he wouldn't get arrested. What came out was the NOVA, and now here we are."

Here we are. Possibly about to trigger a thermonuclear war. Why, oh why, did Dad build that stupid thing? What possible use would he have for it?

"But that still doesn't answer the big question. What happened to make them all hate each other?"

Jai shrugs. "I have no idea. I asked, but my dad won't talk about it. All I know is he thinks your entire family is full of thieves, liars, and traitors. Exact words."

I blink. Thieves, liars, and traitors? That's kind of harsh. And he thinks that about me too? What did I do? "And what do you think?"

"Me? I think..." Jai pauses, mulling over it until the rumbling in the floor stops, and the massive engine buried somewhere in the metal ship powers down. "I think we're here."

"Sir," the intercom buzzes to life, "we've reached our destination."

Jai pushes a button and says, "We'll be right out." Then he turns to me. "You ready?"

I check my waterproof bag, making sure the seal is tight, and nod. "Yeah, let's do this."

With a heave, I sling my bag over my shoulder and head for the torpedo bay.

"Time to go save my dad."

10

The water is inky black, and a cold shiver runs down my spine. I shouldn't be surprised it's this dark, since we're so deep. But knowing is one thing. Actually being submerged is a whole other ball game.

Something moves to my right, and I swing my flashlight over, but nothing's there. Or maybe whatever was there is gone now. I shudder. I don't like the water. I never have. I can swim fine, so it's not a fear of drowning. It's more like…a fear of what's out there in the vast expanse of ocean.

It's the stuff of my nightmares—not just sharks, but sea monsters. Giant, horrifying monsters, with tentacles, and eyes bigger than my entire body. Those giant eyes lurk in the darkness, beyond the reach of my flashlight. Watching. Waiting.

Jai gestures ahead. He points two fingers at his eyes and then one finger in front of him.

I follow his gesture. The "entrance" to the cave is almost invisible. I wasn't expecting neon welcome signs, but it's a crack in the rocks, barely big enough for a person to squeeze through. If he didn't know what to look for, I would've swum right past it. How did Jai find it in the first place?

He swims up to the crack and disappears. Hands shaking, I peer in, shining my flashlight around the interior, but all I see is black. No way. No way am I going in there. But without Jai, I'm all alone in the pitchy ocean, defenseless against the giant monster that's trying to decide which part of me to eat first. I take a deep breath of compressed air and go in after him.

It's like being sucked into a tight black hole. Jagged rocks scrape against my arms and legs, and with every kick my foot collides with the wall. I'm supposed to take long, slow breaths so my lungs don't explode, but instead, my breath sticks in my throat. I hate small spaces. How did my life turn from going to middle school and having no friends to…scuba-diving into tunnels to sneak into a super-villain's lair? All I ever wanted was to be normal. But the normal ship has sailed. Sailed, capsized, and sunk to the bottom of the ocean.

Just when I think I'm about to pass out from claustrophobia, a light flickers ahead. Relieved, I swim toward it.

Jai's already out of the water by the time I surface. He stands on a rock ledge and unstraps his air tank.

He reaches a hand out and pulls me up onto the ledge. I strip off the goggles, the mouthpiece, and the tank that seems to weigh a ton. I never want to do that again.

"You okay?" he says.

"I will be."

Jai picks up his flashlight. "Okay, come on. The entrance is this way."

I adjust my bag and follow him. I'm so glad he had this whole place mapped out ahead of time. This cavern is massive, with no distinguishing features whatsoever. Rock, rock, and more rock. If Jai weren't here, I'd be lost in seconds.

We come to a part of the wall that doesn't look right, like it doesn't belong there. And then I figure out why. The rocks jutting out of the wall aren't natural; they've been placed there.

Jai starts pulling away stones from the middle, revealing a circular opening that's just big enough for us to squeeze through. Despite my hesitation, he pulls me after him, and when the ground underneath us changes from rock to metal grating, it dawns on me that the entrance is so round because it's artificial. We're going through a disguised back door that Jade doesn't know exists.

Now we're in some kind of access tunnel. Copper pipes line one wall, and bundles of electrical wiring line the other. A few feet ahead, the glint of Jai's flashlight beam reveals a ladder. This must be it. This must be the entrance to the pump station.

Jai climbs up and tries to wrench open the manhole cover, but it won't budge. His face whitens.

"Jai, what is it?"

"This shouldn't be bolted shut." He tries again but it still won't move. "This wasn't bolted shut last time."

"What? Let me see."

Jai climbs down and I climb up. Jai's clearly flustered. His plan has barely started and already the wheels are starting to come off.

I push and strain, but he's right. This stupid thing's bolted shut.

He growls, slamming a fist into the metal. "We have to find another entrance."

I'm not listening to him. I'm too busy unzipping my bag and taking out the birthday gift Dad gave me when I turned twelve.

Hot white sparks shower down, and Jai jumps back. My "lipstick" slices through the iron like it's made of tissue paper, and before long it comes loose. With a heave, I manage to push the heavy iron manhole cover open and slide it out of the way.

I looked back down at Jai. "Impressed?"

"Extremely."

Above us is the pump station, as Jai's maps predicted. Immense industrial equipment surrounds us, and its rumbling is earsplitting. The noise makes it the perfect place to break in.

I scan the room with my flashlight. "Looks clear," I whisper.

I scramble up, and Jai climbs after me.

"So, now what?"

Jai leans in, speaking into my ear. "We're really close to the vault. To get there, we take a right out the door, and then a left at the T-junction. But there's a camera there."

I nod. "I'll take care of it."

We sidle up to the door, and I fish through my bag. There's a lot of stuff in there, so it takes me a while to find what I'm looking for, but eventually I pull out one of the headsets made for our Storm Troopers and a small black disk. I snap the headset on and flip the screen down.

"What's that thing?" Jai asks, gesturing at the innocent-looking puck in my hand.

"I'll explain later," I reply, activating it with the push of a button. Carefully, I open the door, slide the device out into the hallway, and fiddle with the controls on my headset, trying to remember which button turns it on.

Okay, don't hit the explode button. Don't hit the explode button.

The screen comes to life. Phew. That would have been embarrassing. Not to mention fatal.

I can see the hallway. It's empty—for now—and in the distance, something is mounted on the wall. A camera, maybe? I fiddle with the controls and my headset zooms in. Yup. Definitely a camera.

I take out my laptop and flip it open. The windows I need appear on the screen. I type "Hello, Camera" and wait, my finger hovering over the enter key as I squint at the screen. The trick is to send the command at the exact moment the camera stops panning to the left and switches direction. There. Command sent.

But nothing happens. Ugh.

"Are you hacking?" Jai whispers excitedly. "You're hacking, aren't you?"

God, I hate that word, "hacking." People assume it's a magical superpower nerds use to make any electronic device do their bidding. Hack that elevator. Hack that toaster. Now let's hotwire that computer to that radio and hack the friggin' moon. Idiots.

A lot of Dad's past remains a mystery to me, but one thing I do know is why he left the Department of Defense. You see, Dad's a brilliant designer and inventor. He didn't just build weapons for the government; he built security systems and body armor. He could build anything they needed, and he did it better than anyone else.

However, the unfortunate thing about working for someone else is that, sometimes, the people in charge aren't always the nicest people in the world. They stole his designs, claimed that they invented them, and there wasn't a thing Dad could do about it because they were in charge.

"Always be the one in charge," Dad used to say, the fires of conviction burning in his eyes. "Always."

I guess that's one of the reasons he's always wanted me to take over the empire. If I'm in charge I won't have to answer to anyone else.

The people who stole his designs sold them for millions, all over the world. Any military base, government installation, heck, even your average mall has his security designs installed. And when Dad became an internationally renowned super-villain, nobody knew it was him who had designed all those security systems. Strange how things work out sometimes.

It's a good thing they didn't know, because in all of Dad's designs, he always made sure to build in a back door.

I type "Hello, Camera" again, this time putting all my concentration into watching that camera, my quivering finger hovering over the Enter key. And this time, I hit it at just the right spot.

"Hello, Manson!" The screen blinks back. I smile. Connection established.

My fingers fly across the keyboard, and soon the camera's looping the last five seconds of footage to whoever's watching the screens. Now we can move, and nobody will know.

Funny. For all our differences, Jai's family and mine finally agree on something. A back door always comes in handy.

I close my laptop and turn to Jai, giving him a thumbs-up. Jai nods, I drop the laptop back into my bag, and we open the door and dash down the hall. The camera continues panning, seeing nothing.

We take a left at the T-junction and soon we're standing in front of Jade's high-security vault.

The thing is massive. Even if I stand on Jai's shoulders, I still won't be able to reach the top of it. Buttons, dials, panels, and iris scanners cover the front. This thing looks as complicated as a super-computer and as impenetrable as Fort Knox.

"You sure you can get this thing open?" Jai asks.

I ignore him, deep in thought. I've spent enough time studying schematics to know that's definitely one of Dad's designs, but which one? I peer at the instruments, whipping through all the schematics in my head. This one has an iris scanner. So is it an MN-603? Or an MN-604?

Footsteps echo down the hall. Someone's coming.

Jai pulls me toward the closest door, and we almost trip over each other, but we make it through just in time. The room is some kind of bathroom, and that's fine with me. I don't care what kind of room it is, as long as we don't get caught.

Jai and I crouch in the dark. The door swings shut but doesn't close completely. A thin sliver of light filters in, between the door and its frame, but we don't dare pull the door shut now.

Whoever he is, he's close enough that we don't hear just his footsteps but also the chatter from his radio, the jostling of the gun at his waist, and the smacking of his lips as he chews gum. For a brief, unbearable second he's right on top of us. And then he moves past, his footsteps receding. Jai and I look at each other and we both release sighs.

But then the door clicks shut.

We hold our breaths and freeze.

The footsteps stop too. Then we hear him turn. He's coming back toward us. His footsteps are slow, wary. I reach out and flip the lock on the door but I know it doesn't matter. If he knows we're in here, we're sunk. If he alerts the rest of the base, Dad's as good as dead.

What do we do? What can we do? Even if we fight our way out, our cover's blown. If our cover is blown, the rescue mission fails. If our rescue mission fails... I don't know what our options are. I don't think we have any.

My stomach leaps into my throat as the door handle rattles.

Jai's expression is grim. He knows we've been caught. He knows there's no way out. But the thing about Jai is he never goes down without a fight. He positions himself behind the door, ready to jump the guard. Hands shaking, I reach into my pocket and take out my lighter.

Some rescue operation this turned out to be. Either we're going to get caught, or we'll have to somehow fight our way out, with all element of surprise flushed down the toilet. Two middle-schoolers against an army of Jade's soldiers. Gee, I wonder who would win that fight?

There's a bang at the door, and we both jump. The guard is trying to kick the door down. The door holds, but we know it won't hold for long.

I look at Jai, and his face is like stone. I wonder what mine looks like. I flick my lighter open.

Just then, when everything seems hopeless, when things couldn't possibly get any worse...

...the base's alarm goes off.

At first, a general alarm goes off, a screaming siren that fills the entire base. Then an electronic voice blares over the speaker system.

"SCRAMBLE. SCRAMBLE. SCRAMBLE."

"Scramble" means "get to your planes" in pilot-speak. I remember hearing that from Mike, but I never did figure out why they don't just say "get to your planes." Pilots are weird, I guess.

In the hallway, I hear lots of running and shouting.

I'm afraid to move, afraid to breathe. I count my own heartbeats, feeling the rush of blood pounding in my ears. I can't count breaths since I'm holding them, and I can't count seconds since I'm too scared to check my watch. So heartbeats it is.

I'm at thirty when I dare to look at the door handle. It's not moving. It's not rattling. In the rush to battle, the guard has forgotten us.

When I let out my breath, it feels like steam bursting out of a kettle.

"That was close," Jai wheezes. All the color had drained from his face, turning his normally cocoa-brown skin a pasty grey.

"Yeah," I gasp. "Too close."

I put my lighter away and glance at my watch. Right on time.

Jim's been itching to hit Jade's base ever since that first attack. By now, a massive wave of Storm Troopers must've charged out of the woods with enough firepower to level everything in their path a hundred times over. I would not want to be the one guarding the west gate right now.

The lights flicker as a distant explosion reverberates through the ground. Concrete trembles beneath my feet. The battle has begun. God only knows who will be left standing when it's all over.

"Come on," Jai hisses at me. "We have to move."

With cautious fingers, he unlatches the door and cracks it open. Jai steels his jaw, ready to pounce on whoever's behind that door, but nobody's there. For now.

Satisfied, he yanks the door open and sneaks into the hallway. I'm right behind him.

The hallways are deserted. All of Jade's men have rushed to stem the tide of Storm Troopers. They must be scared stiff.

"Okay, Sparky," Jai whispers as we sidle up to the safe. "Do your thing."

I examine the door, more closely this time, wracking my brain. Diagrams, schematics, and technical specs whiz around in my head like confetti in a tornado, and I try to catch the right one, but they all move so fast.

Two tumblers—letters and numbers. Iris scanner. Fingerprint scanner. And a voiceprint scanner to boot. This must be the MN-604. No other safe on the planet has this many bells and whistles. No other safe on the planet is this expensive either. Whatever's inside must be valuable.

I whip out the laptop again and set it on the floor. And then I start spinning the safe's tumblers.

6D-61-6E-73-6F-6E.

Bending down, I tap into the keyboard. "Hello, Safe!" And I hit Enter.

Nothing.

"Problem?" Jai whispers. He glances around nervously. He must be expecting a guard to come running at any moment. This is not a good place to have technical problems.

I don't reply. Instead, I clench my jaw, narrow my eyes, and try again.

6D-61-6E-73-6F-6E. It has to be the right combination—the one Dad hid inside this design. Dad made me study those schematics so much I have them memorized. So what's going on?

"Hello, Safe!" Enter.

Nothing.

"Hurry up," Jai says through gritted teeth. He sounds really nervous. "I think I hear someone coming."

Again, I ignore him. I need to think.

Why isn't this working? That's the right combination, I'm sure of it. I search my memory, trying to bring Dad's voice to the surface.

"**I** don't think this is the right combination, Dad," I whined, my fingers working the dials on a prototype in the lab.

Dad looked up from his welding, his blowtorch throwing sparks into the air. "Of course it is. Try it again." He flipped his welding helmet up.

"Why is that the secret combination anyway?" I blew the bangs out of my eyes in frustration. "Did you just pick it randomly?"

"What? No! I never do anything randomly."

"Then why that combination?"

"That," Dad started stroking his goatee, clearly pleased with himself, "is for me to know and you to find out."

I glared at him. "Huh?"

"Think of it as a mystery. A mystery that only an evil genius could ever solve. To figure it out, you'll have to solve a series of puzzles. Evil genius puzzles—each more fiendish than the last."

Ugh. "Stop being so melodramatic."

"Melodramatic?" he said, as if he didn't know what that word meant. "Me?"

I sighed and leaned back in my chair, twirling my hair as I puzzled over the problem. "Let's see, it's a combination of letters and numbers. The numbers are all over the place, but the letters are…not all over the place. D, E, or F. So…maybe they're hexadecimal numbers?"

"Uh…"

I kept going, my mind spinning. "'Isn't that how the ASCII table is arranged?"

"Er…"

Judging by his reaction, I was definitely onto something, so I kept going. "So that means each hexadecimal number represents a letter of the alphabet. So let's see… The first is 6D…and 6D is…" I racked my brain. "6 times 16 is 96…plus 'D'…which is…13…so 109?"

"Well, hold on—"

I ignored him. "And 109 is…'M,' I think…" I suddenly looked over at him. "Does this spell 'Manson' or something?"

Dad stared at me, eyes wide, eyebrows arched so highly they were ready to fly off his head. "Um…I wasn't expecting you to figure that out so fast."

I grinned. "Maybe your puzzles aren't nearly as fiendish as you thought."

"Maybe." Dad stroked his goatee, a smile creeping onto his face. "Or maybe you're turning out to be an evil genius after all."

I squint down at my laptop, plugging numbers into a calculator window. M-a-n-s-o-n. 6D-61-6E-73-6F-6E. That's the right combination. So why isn't it working?

I spin in the numbers again. As fast as I can. I can hear the footsteps coming this way now.

"Hello, Safe!" I type for the third time.

Jai glances back toward the bathroom. I can tell he wants to make a break for it. I'm not sure I want to stay here much longer either. We're both out in the open, totally exposed.

But then, the computer beeps back.

"Hello, Manson!" Third time's the charm.

I let out a sigh of relief. Stupid Dad. He never told me I had to do that three times. I make a mental note. When we're back home, when this is all over, we're going over all these schematics with a fine-toothed comb.

My fingers fly at the keys, and the safe door beeps. One by one, each security system turns green, and finally, the solid-steel, bomb-proof lock disengages with a massive thunk. The safe door swings open.

My heart somersaults in my chest. We made it. We've done it. Dad's right behind this door and he'll know what to do from here on in. I am so ready to retire from all this super-villain stuff. I can hang up my evil cape, and I'll never have to lead another rescue mission again.

Jai seems as eager as I am. Together, we scramble into the safe and pull the door shut. It doesn't lock from the inside, obviously, but anyone passing by won't notice it's unlocked.

Jai and I breathe a sigh of relief.

We did it. We made it. We're safe.

But when I turn around, what I see makes my heart stop.

12

ROWS and rows of bling fill the room. Solid gold bars, containers full of gleaming jewels, all stacked on shelves or piled on tables. In the center, sitting on a plush purple pillow, is the single largest diamond I've ever seen.

Maybe those rumors about Jade and the diamond heist aren't so farfetched after all. The blinding assault by all the sparkle makes it hard for my eyes to adjust, and it takes a while for my mind to connect the dots. This isn't a holding cell. This is a treasure vault.

"Jai? Where's my dad?"

Jai ignores me. He's too busy rummaging through the shelves, tossing aside jewels, gold, and thick wads of cash. He even ignores the fist-sized diamond in the centre of the room.

Something's wrong. A cold, heavy sense of dread in the pit of my gut keeps growing—something's definitely wrong.

"Jai! What's going on?"

He grabs something off one of the shelves and holds it up to the light. It's a silver chain with a strange-looking pendant at the end of it. It has no jewels or diamonds. Compared to the rest of the stuff in this place, it looks relatively worthless.

"What is that?" The pendant looks like a twisty pretzel with a bunch of awkward-looking prongs coming out of one side. Not only is there no bling on it, it isn't even pretty. Why would Jai want that? It's not worth anything. Then it hits me. It's not a pendant.

It's a key.

I stammer, eyes as big as Jade's diamond. "Is that the… NOVA key?"

Jai peers at it. "It looks like it should fit—"

Jai freezes. He's said too much.

He's seen the NOVA.

The voices in my brain clamor to be heard.

But how could Jai have seen the NOVA?

Because he has the NOVA.

Why would Jai have the NOVA?

Because it was his family that kidnapped Dad.

I grab my lighter out of my pocket, but Jai slams into me, rips it out of my hand and sends it clattering to the floor. Then he grabs me by the neck and slams me against the wall.

This can't be happening. Not Jai.

I try to take a swing at him but he sees it coming. Deftly, he moves out of the way and grabs my metallic wrist, twisting my arm and pinning it against my neck. I struggle against him, kicking him as hard as I can in the shins, but it's no use. He's way too strong. I'm completely defenseless.

My eyes refuse to believe what's happening, but my mind reels. The puzzle pieces fall into place, and the plan becomes clear, almost obvious. Too bad I figured it out way too late.

All this time I was blind because of our history, and overwhelmed by everything that had happened, but the signs were there, right in front of me. They assemble, clicking together to form a picture of Jai. Not Jai the protector, nor Jai the savior, but Jai the two-faced, lying scumbag.

He knew too much. He always knew too much, but at no point did I ever think to ask why. He knew we lost the NOVA. He knew right after I got back from that abandoned factory. And he made that joke back in the submarine about the flamethrower strapped to my wrist. How did he know that about it? He had thought this thing was a bionic arm. He even knew my phone got broken in the factory. In fact, he offered to buy me a new one. A bulletproof one. So not only did he know it was broken, he knew it had gotten shot. There's no way anyone could know a detail like that.

Unless he was there.

How could I be so stupid? How could I be so blind? Dad said I was the scorpion, but I'm actually the frog. Don't trust anyone. That's the lesson I should've taken away from that story. And now it's too late. I'm alone, trapped where nobody can save me.

"You..." My voice shakes. It doesn't even sound like me. So much rage and adrenaline courses through my veins I can't see straight. "You can't activate it without my key."

Jai smirks. The sideways smirk I used to know so well now seems cruel, twisted.

"You have no idea what the keys are, do you?" he says. "The keys are all different. Only Jade's is an actual, physical key. Ours is an iris scan. And yours?" He reaches into his pocket and takes out a syringe. "It's a blood sample."

"Hold still." He uncaps it using his teeth, revealing a long needle, and the moment I see it I struggle, trying to break his grip, but he slams me against the wall again. "Hold. Still," he repeats, fire burning in his pale blue eyes.

I can't take my eyes off the needle as he brings it closer. "Jai... Wait... I..."

And then he plunges it into my arm.

I yelp as the needle goes in. It only lasts a second, but that second seems to stretch for hours. When he pulls it out, the syringe is filled with my blood.

Jai releases me, and I fall to the floor. My hand flies to my arm. It's small, but it hurts. When I bring my hand up to my face, blood coats my fingers.

Uncle Tom's voice echoes in my head. *He was adamant that Fiona take over. He said something like "blood is everything."*

I'm paralyzed, like a computer with a virus. My blood is the third key.

Jai picks something up off the floor. "This is a nice lighter." He whistles, as if impressed. "Thanks." He slips it, along with the syringe of my blood, into his pocket and salutes me. "Later, Sparky."

"Jai, wait," I call out.

Jai stops at the vault door, turning around. He looks like he's expecting something. Maybe he's expecting me to fall apart. Maybe he's expecting me to go down on my hands and knees and beg him not to leave me.

Instead, I whip a vase at him.

He ducks at the last second, and it shatters into a million priceless pieces behind him.

"You were supposed to be my friend!" I scream.

"I'm a super-villain, Sparky. Super-villains don't have friends." Jai smirks again.

Sparky. If I didn't hate that name before, I hate it so much now that hearing it makes me want to hack his face off with a machete. I trusted him. I trusted him when I didn't even trust Jim or Uncle Tom. How could I have been so wrong?

He swings open the vault door, and, to my surprise, I call out after him. "Bad guys always die at the end." That makes him pause, so I keep going. "You should remember that."

He takes one last look at me through those weird blue eyes and says, "You're a bad guy too."

Then he leaves, shutting the vault behind him.

I run to the door as the impenetrable locks re-engage. "Jai! Jai!" I pound on the door, but it's no use. There's no way to unlock an MN-604 from the inside. Not with dynamite, not with hacking, not with anything. I'm trapped.

I keep pounding until my fists ache, and yet I keep on. I'm out of ideas and out of options. Pounding on that twelve-inch steel is the thing I have left, even though I know it's not going to work. Nobody's coming to rescue me. Nobody knows I'm here.

Uncle Tom probably thinks I've reached the jail cells and I'm already on my way back with Dad in tow. And Jim? He's probably still fighting Jade's soldiers at the west gate. His orders are to attack, not to protect me.

With no one watching, I finally break down. I collapse against one of the metal shelves, sobbing.

Every decision I've made has been a complete, unmitigated disaster. It was my decision to hand over the NOVA. It was my decision to attack Jade. And it was my decision to trust Jai.

Jai. I always knew he was a bully and a jerk but that was always to other people. Never to me. He would never stuff me into a locker, I always told myself. Now I wish he had. Maybe if he had, I wouldn't be here, trapped in a vault, feeling like someone had just shot a giant hole through my chest.

I let our friendship cloud my judgment. That's it, plain and simple. Why else did I trust him so blindly? Why else did I rest all my hopes for rescuing Dad on a kid from a rival family?

I let them all down in the end. My family, my home, my empire. I bury my face in my hands, letting the tears fall where they want to. I don't care anymore. I lost. I may as well cry. It's not like I can sink any lower.

A beep interrupts my sobs. An electronic beep coming from the MN-604.

The sound of the vault door's tumblers snapping into place fills the room and, with a hiss and a thunk, the locks disengage. I leap to my feet as the door swings open. Is it one of the good guys or one of the bad guys? Do I even know who is who anymore?

My questions are answered by the ominous sound of heavy combat boots. And by the grim glare of fiery red eyes.

Ruby stares at me. "What are you doing here?

Ruby does not look happy to see me. To be fair, Ruby never looks happy to see anyone, but right now she looks apocalyptic. Those crimson eyes are glowing with rage. Hopefully it's regular rage, rather than the murderous kind.

"Ruby, wait," I stammer. "We have bigger problems right now."

"We?" Ruby says, like she's playing with the word on her silver-pierced tongue. "Who's we?"

She takes a step closer.

"Ruby," I hold out my hands. "Jai has the NOVA."

"Jai has the NOVA? Oh no. Jai has the NOVA!" She's mocking me. Her pale white face is only inches from mine. "What the heck is a NOVA?"

I give myself a mental head slap. She doesn't know.

I'm trapped here, the NOVA's on its way back to The Captain, and Ruby has no idea how serious the situation is.

I am in huge trouble.

As if on cue, Ruby wraps an arm around my neck, pulls me toward her, and slams her knee into my stomach.

I double over, groaning, and drop to the ground. But she's not done with me. She's just getting started.

Ruby hauls me back up and slams a fist into my temple. Crazy colors and shapes spin around me as the world goes sideways. I'm on the ground, writhing in pain. The pain is so intense I can't move, speak, or even think. The pain is all that exists.

"Still think I fight like a girl?"

She winds back and slams one of her boots into my chest. I scream. The impact sends a blinding jolt of agony through me, and my lungs feel like they're on fire. She literally knocked the breath out of me.

The agony crushes me, pins me to the floor, and a hot tear rolls down my cheek as I struggle to breathe through my burning lungs. Each breath is torture.

But she doesn't seem to care. A smile creeps across her face as she watches me contort.

I am so completely and utterly doomed.

She raises a walkie-talkie to her lips. "Ruby to Jade. Come in, Jade."

A crackle of static. "What is it? We're kind of busy right now—" I can hear the sound of gunfire in the background.

"I found someone in the vault you might be interested in."

"So take care of it."

"It's Fiona. Manson's kid."

Silence. "We'll be right down."

Ruby clicks off the radio, giving me a satisfied look. "They'll be right down."

I grit my teeth and pull myself up. "Ruby," I gasp. "You have to listen to me. Jai tricked me. I thought your family kidnapped my dad."

"Stop with the lies, Fiona. You're better than that."

"I'm not lying. This entire attack was supposed to be a rescue mission."

"A rescue mission?" she spits back through clenched teeth. "I don't believe you. If this is a rescue mission, then why are you in our vault?"

I open my mouth but nothing comes out. Because…I thought you were keeping my dad in here? God, it sounds so stupid when I say it like that. Why did I trust Jai's plan so blindly? Why did I trust Jai so blindly?

"You know," Ruby shakes her head sadly, "for the longest time, I really thought you were one of the good guys. The only one out of the three of us that would get out from under the shadows of our parents."

She takes a step forward, a strange look in her blood-hued eyes. I've never seen that look before, and it scares the living crap out of me.

"Jai was a lost cause," she says, waving a hand in the air. "Jai was stuffing kids into garbage cans on his first day of kindergarten. But me? I wanted to be a good guy, too. You know, like you."

I respond to that strange look in her eyes with one of my own. This is all news to me. For as long as I could remember, Ruby hated me with a passion.

"Do you remember when we met?"

I shake my head.

"I walked into class, that first day, and immediately, before I did or said anything, everyone took one look at me and screamed." Ruby gestures at her ivory skin. "Because of this. And because of..." She closes her eyes for a moment, seemingly fighting back tears. But when she opens them, they harden into stone. "...this."

I start to understand. Her eyes are the first thing most people notice. They make her look alien. They make her look scary. They make her look...

...evil.

"And that's when I realized I can never be the good guy. Everyone looks at me and sees a villain. And that's—" she laughs now, a cold, hollow laugh "—that's okay. I've accepted that. But you—" she jabs a black fingernail at me. "I expected you to understand. I expected you to know what's it's like to be different. I expected you to know what it's like to be alone."

I stare back, wide-eyed, a million images flashing through my head. I do remember that first day now. I remember seeing Ruby for the first time. Like everyone else, I was scared of her pale skin and her red eyes. I thought she was a demon, or possessed, or a ghost. But come on. I was five! She can't possibly hold that against me.

Can she?

"It's funny, actually." She laughs that empty laugh again. "Look at you. Attacking our base. Stealing from our vault. Turns out you aren't the good guy after all. You're just another villain. Like me."

I balk. That's why she thinks I'm in here? That I'm a common thief?

The heavy metal vault door behind us swings open with a creak. Cue ominous music.

A man and a woman enter. The man has a military buzz-cut, and he's wearing some kind of grey-and-white uniform. The woman has flowing hair, down to her waist. They share Ruby's same blood-red eyes and translucent hair.

Jade and Hawk haven't been seen in public for years, and the photos our intel people have are at least eight years old. But it has to be them. No other two people could look so imposing.

Hawk whistles. "Well, well, well…"

"…look who we have here," Jade chimes in.

The way they complete each other's sentences is something I remember reading about in our reports, but it seems no less weird in person.

"It's a pleasure to finally meet you," Jade coos at me, all motherly, but her words only send a shiver down my spine.

She gestures to the cadre of guards around her, and they rush up and grab me. "Wait!" I try to shout, but duct tape is wrapped around my mouth, and my arms are wrenched behind my back. They drag me away. I have no idea whether it's toward a jail cell, toward a torture chamber, or toward a shallow grave, but my mind's racing, thinking of all the horrible possibilities. Is this it? Did I barely survive Ruby only for it all to end like this? It seems so unfair. So…anti-climactic.

"Did she say anything?" I hear Hawk ask as they drag me out of the vault.

"She said lots of stuff." Ruby shrugs. "Something about Jai. Something about her dad. Something about a NOVA—"

"Wait…" Hawk starts.

"…what?" Jade finishes.

Ruby freezes. The guards freeze. Everyone freezes. I hold my breath, counting my heartbeats as my eyes flit among the three of them.

Hawk runs to a spot on the shelves, toppling over a few bars of silver on his way. He goes to the same spot where Jai found the NOVA key and, after a few seconds of frantic digging, turns back to Jade, looking somehow even paler.

Jade is stone-faced, all her smugness gone. She strides up to me, bends down, and rips off the tape. I yelp, but she doesn't notice. Or care. "Where's the NOVA?" she demands.

"Jai," I gasp. "Jai has it."

"And the keys?"

"Jai has them."

"How many?" There's something different in Jade's eyes, and it takes me a second to place it. It's not smugness or cruelty. It's…desperation. "How many?"

I lick my parched lips, my face still burning. "All of them."

Helicopters flood the air, buzzing like massive, metallic mosquitoes.

"You owe us a new gate," Hawk grumbles.

"Oh, shut up," Jim growls back, adjusting his eyepatch.

After the confrontation in the vault, Jade handed me a radio, and I ordered an immediate cease-fire. The attack is over. Now both sides are bruised and battered, trying to figure out what happened.

Behind us, the west gate lies in ruin, destroyed and indefensible. The only thing left is a single brick arch, barely hanging on. If I hadn't ordered the ceasefire, the Storm Troopers would've quickly overrun the base. However, I'm not about to say that. There aren't many reasons for either side to gloat right now.

"You Neanderthals couldn't have figured out whether your precious boss was even here before you destroyed half our base?" Hawk yells over the sound of thumping helicopter blades.

Jim turns. "What did you just call us?"

I step between the two. "Guys. Guys. Bigger problems at hand. Remember?"

The two back down, but not before shooting murderous looks at each other.

One of our helicopters touches down in front of us, and a familiar figure steps out. His trademark pinstriped dress shirt and silver-rimmed glasses look completely out of place in a combat zone.

"Jade, Hawk." Uncle Tom nods curtly at them. "It's been a long time."

Hawk doesn't look the least bit happy to see him. "Yes…"

"…it has," Jade finishes.

Pleasantries aside (if you can call them that), Uncle Tom turns toward me, all businesslike. "How long has Jai been gone?"

"About thirty minutes."

"And what's he in?"

"A submarine."

Uncle Tom turns to Jade. "A submarine. That would take, what, an hour or so to get back to his dad's armada?" Nods all around. "So that means we have half an hour before he gets back to the NOVA with all the keys. We have to stop him before then."

"And how are you planning on doing that?" Jim interrupts. "With more negotiations?"

"No." Uncle Tom glares at him. "I propose an all-out joint aerial assault on that battleship."

Jim gives him a strange look. A tiny smile pulls at the corner of his mouth. "Finally. Something we can agree on."

Something shifts among us. Suddenly we aren't warring factions anymore. The threat of a thermonuclear bomb makes us all equally doomed, and that simple fact puts us all on the same side. At least temporarily.

"Jade." Uncle Tom turns to our former enemy. "The Captain's armada has some top-notch air defenses. Can you take them out?"

Hawk answers, a huge smirk on his face. "Oh, yeah. They'll never know what hit them."

Jade jumps in. "And what about afterward?"

"Then we land our Storm Troopers," Uncle Tom says. "We'll capture the ship, we'll capture Jai, and then we'll capture the NOVA."

"You sure these Neanderthals can pull this off?" Hawk says, rolling his eyes.

As if on cue, the brick arch collapses behind us, showering Jade's repair crews with smoky debris. Smugly, Jim turns back toward Hawk. "You get us on that ship. We'll take care of the rest."

"**You** fly Fiona straight home and stay there, okay?" Jade shouts over the din. Around us, armored helicopters spool up, and soldiers run back and forth across the tarmac. Some are ours, some are theirs, and they're all scrambling to get ready for what will probably be the biggest battle anyone's ever seen in their life.

"Okay," Ruby shouts back as she climbs into one of our helicopters. "Don't worry about us."

However, before I climb in after her, I spot Jim directing some soldiers to their attack craft. "Jim!" I call out.

"What?" he calls back.

"Can I borrow a lighter? Jai stole mine."

He turns to his men. "Hey! Do any of you guys have a lighter?"

One of them replies, "Here!" He tosses something to Jim, who tosses it to me. This old, dented Zippo isn't my fancy gold-plated lighter, but at least it makes fire. It'll have to do for now.

I climb into the helicopter with Ruby and strap myself into the co-pilot's seat. A million buttons and dials cover the dashboard in front of me, and I have no idea what any of them mean. Fortunately, Ruby seems to. As she starts jabbing buttons and flipping switches, the main rotor above us starts to spin up.

"You're not planning on taking me back home, are you?" I ask.

"Not a chance. You think I'm going to miss this?" Ruby turns to me, her vivid eyes shining even brighter than normal. "This might be the only chance we'll ever get to be the good guys for once."

I smile at that. I can't help it.

"And besides," Ruby says, "you weren't planning on sitting this one out either."

I raise my eyebrows. "What do you mean?"

We put on our headphones as the other helicopters' main rotors spin up. "Why else would you ask for that lighter?"

As I flick the Zippo with my thumb, a grin stretches across my face. She's right. I have no intention of going home either.

Ruby continues flicking switches and pushing buttons as our main rotor gets louder.

"Um, Ruby?" I say into the microphone, my hollow voice reflecting back into my headset. "Are you sure you know how to fly this thing?"

Ruby turns to me with an incredulous expression, as if I asked the dumbest question ever. And then, still glaring at me, she pulls open the throttle and executes a perfect liftoff.

It's a beautiful day, clear blue sky in all directions and not a cloud visible. The sun begins its lazy descent into the west, sinking gradually to kiss the horizon behind us. It really is a perfect day.

A perfect day for a helicopter attack.

The thwup-thwup-thwup of the blades fills the air around me, but for some reason I don't feel like I'm on a helicopter at all. Ruby is flying this thing like an absolute pro. I should know. I've ridden to school in helicopters since I was five, but the ride has never been this smooth. From our spy reports, I know that Ruby's a great pilot, but this? This is something else. It's like she's one with the helicopter.

"How do you know how to fly this thing?"

"If it flies, I can fly it." She shrugs. "And besides, helicopters are easy. I could pilot this thing with my eyes closed. Now, jet fighters, those are tricky. Have you ever flown in a jet fighter?"

I shake my head. "Nope, can't say that I have." I've never even sat in one.

"Let me tell you, you haven't lived until you've done a high-G barrel roll in one of those things. That's how I earned my wings. I should take you sometime."

"Uh…I don't think so." I gag. That sounds just awful.

A high-G barrel roll? I don't even know what high-G means, but if Ruby's excited about it, I probably want as few of those "Gs" as humanly possible. I don't even like roller coasters. Jet fighter? No way. Besides, the pilot's vision would quickly be obscured by me filling the cockpit with vomit.

"Wait, what do you mean when you say you earned your wings?" I ask.

"That's just a pilot saying," Ruby says. "When you've gotten good enough to fly on your own, we say you've earned your wings. It's kind of a big deal for us, like a rite of passage. They give you a call sign, and from then on that's what everyone calls you. It's your new name. Forever and ever."

Huh. I always thought that whole call sign thing was kind of lame. I'd no idea they took them that seriously. A rite of passage. That's actually kind of cool. "How old were you when you got your wings?"

"Eight."

The helicopter tilts to the left as we bank away from the course that would take us to my volcano home and head toward the rest of the attack force.

It's horribly risky, but for me there is no other option. The Storm Troopers are all flying gleefully into danger for my family. I can't sit at home with my fingers crossed, hoping they make it out alive. That's not my style. I have to be with them every step of the way.

But Ruby? I have a sneaking suspicion she just wants to blow stuff up.

"So how big of a bomb is this NOVA thing?" Ruby asks.

"Um, let's see." I struggle to remember Uncle Tom's words. "About a hundred times as powerful as the bomb that was dropped on Hiroshima."

"Oh." She pauses, hesitating. "So if it goes off—"

"You, me, and this entire city—vaporized."

She looks sullen. "You don't think he'll actually set it off, do you?"

I shake my head. "I have no idea. Jai's dad is pretty unpredictable. Remember the time that cruise liner cut him off and he threatened to torpedo it?"

Ruby nods. "How do you even 'cut someone off' in the middle of the ocean anyway?"

"I know, right?" I start to laugh, but then stop myself. This is so weird. Here we are, joking like best friends, but not long ago Ruby slammed a fist into the side of my head. Heck, even now the boot-shaped bruise she gave me is throbbing. "Why did your family attack our base, Ruby?"

Ruby shrugs. "I don't know, exactly. It wasn't my decision."

Isn't that what bad guys always say? That it wasn't their idea? But Ruby continues, oblivious. "I don't think we were trying to kill you or your dad. I think we just wanted to send a message so you wouldn't mess with us." Her eyes flit to the floor in embarrassment. "We didn't know that Jai was watching."

"Don't feel too bad. Jai duped us both." I crack my metallic knuckles. "Well, now I guess it's time to return the favor, right?"

She flashes me a red laser-beam glare. "Right."

Up ahead, a cloud of black-and-red dots putters through the cerulean sky. It's our helicopters. We're catching up to the attack force. The radio suddenly crackles to life. "Ruby? What are you doing?"

Right on cue.

Ruby pushes the transmit button. "We're joining the attack."

Jade screeches, "Absolutely not. You're supposed to be heading to safety!"

I push the transmit button. "Jade, with all due respect, there is no safety. Not with the NOVA in play." I briefly flash back to the warehouse, when I finally made that decision to stop cowering in the corner and start throwing fireballs. I'm never ever going back to cowering again. "At least this way, if we have to go down, we can go down fighting."

Ruby flashes me a thumbs-up. *Nice,* she mouths.

A long pause, a long crackle of static. "You will head back to the air base immediately and stand down, Ruby."

"That's a negative," Ruby says.

"You are so getting grounded when this is all over. I mean it. No flying for a year."

Ruby's eyes go wide, and I can't help but snicker. For any other family, grounding means staying in your room and never going out. But for a family of pilots? It literally means something so much worse.

"I don't care," Ruby finally says. "This is too important. You can either help us or you can leave us exposed."

A pause. A really long pause. The terrain below us changes from forested mountains to turquoise water before Ruby turns to me. "You don't think she's actually going to ground me for a year, do you?"

I shrug, shaking my head. How would I know? If I was Jade, I wouldn't ground my best pilot, but I'm not her.

Slowly, some of the black-and-red dots veer away from the group and circle back toward us.

Ruby breathes an audible sigh of relief. They're not going to leave us exposed. We can't know what will happen when the guns go off, but at least we're not alone. We have an entire army with us.

The awesome sight of the squadron jogs my memory. I dig in the compartment underneath my seat.

C'mon. Where is it? I could have sworn it's in here somewhere.

Ruby looks over, puzzled. "What are you looking for?"

I dig up a silver disc. "This."

Dad always made me promise to play it if we ever managed to get into this situation. In fact, that's why he had these giant external speakers installed in the first place. For this exact situation.

"You're going to play music?" Ruby shouts as I slide the CD into a slot on the dashboard.

"Dad made me promise," I say.

"But…but…won't they hear us coming?"

"Ruby," I look at her, "do you really think they don't already know?"

She stops and considers it. "I guess not." And then she scowls at me. "But you don't have to be so…melodramatic."

"Melodramatic?" I say, flabbergasted. "Me?"

The music comes on, and the little LCD screen reads, "Ride of the Valkyries." I have no idea what that song is, but the minute it starts blaring, I know why Dad picked it. It's something Death would have on his iPod playlist, like something the Four Horsemen of the Apocalypse would play from their stereo. It's so ominous. So menacing. So...

Deliciously evil.

Now, I'll admit, I'm not the most experienced villain, to say the least. This is the first time I've ever tried to attack anything in my entire life. But right now, with my Storm Troopers flying beside me, my flamethrower strapped to my wrist, and evil-sounding music blaring from my armored attack helicopter, I feel like a proper super-villain.

The weirdest part?

It feels kind of good.

The trumpets blare triumphantly on the soundtrack as my attack force forms around us. My family's black-and-red assault craft fall into formation. Ruby's family's nimble white helicopters form a shield in front of us. We're like a flock of metallic hovering birds, with enough combined firepower to level a mountain.

I can't believe all of this is actually happening. A single tear rolls down my cheek. "It's so beautiful, Dad," I whisper. "I wish you could be here to see this."

Maybe I'm not that bad at this whole super-villain thing after all.

But then, as if the tiny bud of relief is too ridiculous for the universe to handle, a shape starts to form. At first, I'm not sure if it's a ship, an island, or a volcano, but as we get closer, the sharp angles and the blinking lights confirm it's a ship, the biggest ship I've ever seen in my life.

"Holy crap," Ruby says, taking the words right out of my mouth. "That's what we're trying to take down?"

I gape. How the heck are we going to take that thing out? It's a floating city with more weaponry than most military bases. Massive gun turrets stretch into the sky like skyscrapers amidst an island of grey steel. Dozens of smaller ships—destroyers, frigates, and cruisers—surround the floating city. I can already see the rocket launchers on the battleship swiveled in our direction.

Beep! Beep! Beep!

The alarms shriek as the rockets come barreling at us. White vapor trails fill the sky, and my heart races. There are so many. Too many to count. The radio explodes in loud chatter.

"Incoming ordnance."

"Locking on."

"Open fire!"

Jade's white helicopters launch rockets of their own. While the battleship missiles are big, heavy, and slow, Jade's are small, nimble, and quick. They zigzag in the air as they zero in, slamming into the incoming projectiles in spectacular walls of fire. "Ride of the Valkyries" blares on, glorious and triumphant.

Before my next breath, the cockpit fills with beeping alarms again. Another barrage launches toward us. This time, it's not just from the battleship; it's also from all the smaller ships. "There's too many!" someone shouts over the radio.

"Take them out!" another voice responds.

Another barrage of rockets and wall of fire burst in front of us, only this time, our alarm is still blaring. One of theirs made it through, and it's coming straight for us.

"Hold onto something!" Ruby yells. I white-knuckle my armrest as Ruby flips the helicopter upside-down.

We twist so fast my head smashes into the window. No matter how good of a pilot you think you are, helicopters just don't like to be upside-down.

Through the windshield, I see the water and the sky fight over what gets to be on top, but I'm too busy screaming to pick a winner. The only things I know are that my stomach slams into my heart, my heart slams into my throat, and my internal organs slam into each other like a horrible internal-organ milkshake. I would throw up if I weren't afraid my liver would come flying out.

But then Ruby rights the helicopter. The sky and water resume their correct positions, and the monitor shows the missile spiraling uselessly into the water below us.

"Never do that again!" I scream at Ruby, but she can't hear me over her laughter. Clearly, she's having the time of her life.

Me? Not so much. All around us is pure, unadulterated chaos. Helicopters buzz in every direction. Some mine, some Jade's. And every few seconds, hot rockets whiz past, narrowly missing our aircraft and almost incinerating a squad of our men. How long can we hang on? How long until something horrible happens?

Thankfully, I don't have to witness the answer to that question. The familiar sound of a banshee fills the air as Jade's silver dive-bombers swoop down like vengeful angels.

My instincts tell me to run, remembering that sound from the attack on my volcano home. The high-pitched whine is scary. Incredibly scary. And it suddenly dawns on me—it's supposed to scare the pants off people. That's the entire point.

As the silver planes zero in on their targets, people run for cover; they look like little blue dots, diving for their lives.

Three destroyers explode into infernos, fire engulfing their decks as elated whooping blasts from the radio.

"Woooo!"

"Burn, baby, burn!"

The missiles continue sailing in from every direction, their white vapor trails crisscrossing like steaming dragons. Ruby ignores the chaos, yanking the stick forward, and our helicopter charges toward one of the ships. Acceleration pushes me back against my seat, and it's all I can do to stare, open-mouthed, as one of the warships looms closer and closer in our windscreen. Ruby presses a button and sends a barrage of rockets to carpet its deck. As we pass over it, the destroyer is consumed by fire and smoke.

All around us, the scene repeats. We couldn't hit Jade's aircraft when they attacked us, and Jai's family can't either. The fighting is fierce, but gradually the odds shift in our favor.

Eventually, their guns fall silent, blown into twisted wreckage, while ours keep firing.

Jade's air force really is unbeatable. Like hornets, they swarm and sting, a cloud of pain, but with missiles instead of stingers. Yet they're so fast nothing can hit them. Shooting at them is like firing a machine gun into a hissing cloud. You hit nothing, and the hornets just get angrier and send out more stinging missiles.

As if to prove my point, another detonation envelops The Captain's battleship, as three glinting dive-bombers scream away into the clouds.

Ruby and I watch in awe as smoke pours from the wounded behemoth. All we hear now is the thumping of our helicopter's blades and the music blaring from our speakers. It takes me a moment to realize what that means—the ships aren't shooting at us anymore.

My watch beeps. Thirty minutes.

Uncle Tom's voice rings in my head. We have half an hour before Jai reaches the armada.

Our time is up.

I have no idea whether our attack delayed Jai or if he's already on board, but time's up. With their air defenses down, we now have the chance to save the world, so to speak.

"What now?" Ruby asks.

"Get me on that ship."

"You sure?" Ruby bites her lip. "I don't know. It still looks pretty dangerous down there. Maybe we should—"

"You guys have done enough." I unbuckle my seat belt. "Let us do our part."

I get up and position myself by the door. The battleship billows smoke, but already I see the blue dots massing on the main deck, guns bristling. They know we're going to board. They know we're going to invade. And they're not going to go down without a fight.

Gut check, Fiona. Gut check. Am I a frog, or am I a scorpion?

I jam on my headset. "Jim? Are we ready to board?"

A crackle of static. "We? What do you mean, we? You're not coming!"

"I absolutely am," I say, rolling my eyes. "We've been over this. I'm not sending anyone into danger without going in myself."

"You're going to get shot at pretty severely down there, Fiona."

"We're Storm Troopers, Jim," I say, a smile slowly spreading upon my lips. "We're supposed to get shot at."

A pause. And when Jim speaks again, I can picture his expression. "You know, if I ever have a kid, I hope she's half as awesome as you."

Flicking the Zippo, I bring the flame to my wrist. With a woomf, the flamethrower lights off, its blue liquid coursing through the tube like the fury coursing through my veins. The ship is getting close now. Here we go.

"Where do you want me to land?" Ruby calls out.

Taking a deep breath, I pull open the side door, and immediately the blue men start firing. Flashes of white erupt from all over the ship's deck, and bullets ping off the helicopter's armor. I don't even flinch.

Instead, I wind my arm back and send a massive screaming fireball down toward the center of the deck. The explosion scatters the blue people like terrified ants. I turn to Ruby, pointing at the scorched crater I just made.

"Right there."

The deck steadies in front of us, and I'm not afraid anymore. I feel nothing. A few days ago, I would've curled up in a corner, shaking uncontrollably, paralyzed by indecision. But now? It's like I've forgotten to bring my fear. I've stuffed it in my lunch box back home. It's a weird feeling. But I'm glad it's there. All my regret and hesitation has disappeared. Once the helicopter touches metal, I'll be ready.

As I'm about to jump out, Ruby says something that makes me stop: "Good luck, Fireball."

"Fireball?" I look back at her. "What is that? My call sign?"

She smiles, nodding. "Yeah. You like it?"

I smile. I do like it.

Fireball. I could get used to that.

My black-and-red helicopters touch down with us. Storm Troopers flood out like righteous vengeance. I feel the fury my soldiers have been bottling up—the fury that aches for sweet, fiery release.

We're called the Storm Troopers because we love storming things. And this is our chance. Now we can be the invaders.

And it feels So. Freaking. Good.

Gunfire fills the air, and bullets ping off the deck around me, but I step out anyway.

We swarm the deck so fast nothing seems able to hit us.

I close my eyes, breathing in the scent of gunfire, seawater, and fires burning out of control (some made by yours truly), and I smile. My flamethrower hums hungrily, begging to do some damage. And who am I to argue with such a request?

"Hang on, Dad. The Bad Guys are coming."

My presence in the raging battle generates mostly confusion. Every so often, a gaggle of blue-uniformed men charges out of a doorway, spots me, and freezes. They stare, looking dumbfounded, probably wondering what a kid is doing in the middle of a firefight.

However, when I send a looming wall of fire roaring at them, their confusion erupts into panic. Never underestimate the power of fear. Jade knows how to wield it from the air, and now I know how to wield it on the ground.

I peer through the growing cloud of smoke enveloping the deck, trying to spot Jim. All around me I hear the rat-a-tat-a-tat of machine guns and the deep throaty pow-pow-pow of our guns returning fire. I'm not as scared as I thought I'd be. At this point it seems almost…normal.

That's probably not a good thing.

I spot Jim in the distance, through the haze and smoke. He's huddled behind a crate, along with a squad of my Storm Troopers, firing upward.

Blue men fire back at him from a balcony. Jim's squad doesn't seem able to hit them from where they are, but the blue men can rain fire down on them from relative safety.

But not for long.

I whip out a fireball and it slams into the bulkhead behind the blue men, exploding in a spectacular blaze. Two men screech as they dive over the railings toward the water, limbs flailing.

Jim looks at me and smiles, flashing a thumbs-up. Everyone gets on their feet and advances toward the grey superstructure housing the guts of the battleship. Jim pumps his fist up and down in the air. Move, move, move! The Storm Troopers form up behind him, seemingly glad to have the chance to live up to their nickname.

Jim yanks open a metal door and enters the superstructure, the rest, including me, following close behind as one cohesive unit. We surge into claustrophobic halls that smell of sweat and gunpowder. We surge deep into the core of the ship, sending bursts of automatic fire in every direction as we push the blue men back. The explosive shots from our guns echo through the halls. My heart jackhammers, my pulse pounds, but I don't care. I've never felt so alive.

The squad charges forward while I follow behind, watching the rear. My flamethrower growls. If anyone tries to sneak up behind us, they're so getting charbroiled.

"Yo, Major," one of the Storm Troopers calls out, causing the whole team to stop, their guns jostling.

"What?"

"Check it." He gestures toward a sign with an arrow pointing to the left. *Weapons Lab.*

Everyone's thinking the same thing. That's got to be where Dad is. Any weapons lab is practically his second home.

Jim nods, and we move as one. I pity whoever makes the terrible decision to step in front of us. I also think about what will happen if anyone steps in front of my flamethrower. I can't decide which is worse.

We form up against a metal door at the end of the corridor. Next to it, a sign reads *Weapons Lab.* I take a deep breath. Please let Dad be in there.

Jim holds out a gloved hand and everyone gets ready. One. Two. Three. Go.

We burst into the lab, weapons raised, ready to shoot, but we don't find Dad. A scared-looking egghead in a white lab coat stares back at us.

Jim grabs him. "Where's Manson?" he demands.

"What? I...I don't—"

Jim jams his weapon into the egghead's collarbone. "Where is he?"

"I...don't..." he stammers. "I don't know who you're talking about."

Ugh. This guy's a worse liar than I am. And as much fun as it would be to watch Jim beat the answers out of him, we just don't have time. I push my way to the front.

"Listen to me," I say, making each syllable count. The man's silver hair is the same shade as his wire-rimmed glasses frame. He's easily five times older than me, but I have his rapt attention. "You have my dad. I want him back."

Whoa. Who is this person talking? I sound scary.

"Tell me where he is." My eyes bore into him. "Tell me where he is, or something very, very bad is going to happen to you." I take a step forward, flexing my metallic fingers. "Got it?"

The egghead looks at Jim, then at me, then back at Jim. "Is she serious?"

I point to a nearby workbench. The jet of orange flame is so hot, the glassware on the bench explodes, popping like shrapnel-filled popcorn. The table itself ignites, throwing hot orange flames toward the ceiling.

I turn my gaze back on Egghead, my face hard as stone. "Do I look serious now?"

Egghead stares at me, his eyes flitting between me and the blaze that was once his table. "He—he's in the brig."

I try my best not to show it, but inside I'm pumping my fist in the air, screaming with happiness. That means Dad's okay. We can still rescue him.

Jim doesn't show it either, even though I know he's as happy as I am. After all, the sooner we get Dad back, the sooner I don't have to be in charge. It's a win-win. Like a poker player, Jim scowls, jamming his gun into Egghead's temple.

"Take us there."

The gunmetal hallways look identical and endless. If I were in front, I wouldn't have the slightest idea where to go, but Egghead seems to know, so we follow. People with guns jammed in their temples tend not to lie.

"This way." Egghead points to a hallway on our right, and Jim pivots the team. His assault rifle is up, ready to take down anyone who stands in his way, but nobody comes.

We line up behind a metal door. This is it. This is the place. A sign by the door reads "Brig."

Jim holds up a gloved hand, once again. One. Two. Three. Go.

The Storm Troopers burst in and I follow behind. We expect a fight. We expect an army. But somehow, the room is empty. Abandoned. Nobody's there, except for...Dad.

He sits in his cell, a cast over his right arm. The moment he sees us, he's on his feet.

"Major," he says, a relieved grin spreading across his face. "You have no idea how happy I am to see you."

"Likewise, sir." Jim says, always calm, always professional. "What happened to your arm?"

"Oh, that happened when they grabbed me back at the base." He waves his good arm dismissively. "I'll be fine."

I burst forward, past the uniforms. "Dad!"

It's him. It's really him! And he's okay!

I reach through the bars and give him the biggest bear hug ever. I wrap my arms around his neck, and tears of relief cascade down my cheeks like hot waterfalls.

"Uh...Fiona?" Jim taps my shoulder. "I think you're choking him."

"Huh?" I let go and Dad collapses to one knee, gasping for breath. Right. Metal arm. I have to watch that. "Er...love you?"

"Love..." Dad coughs, still rubbing his neck. "...you too, Honey."

"Major?" one of the Storm Troopers calls out, "they took the keys. I can't find them." On the abandoned guard's desk are handcuffs and batons, but no keys.

It doesn't ruffle Jim in the least. "Sir, stand back. We're going to blow it open."

Dad backs away and tips his bed on its side to use it as a shield. I try to stay calm but my hands shake. I'm no expert on explosives, but I'm pretty sure that flimsy little mattress isn't going to do much to protect him.

However, it doesn't really matter what I think. A Storm Trooper is already wiring up the cell door.

It's a delicate job. Too little and we don't blow the lock. Too much and we liquefy Dad. But I have to trust my men at this point. They've gotten us this far, haven't they?

As much as I try to keep my nerves in check, my panic seems to boil over as he gets ready to set off the explosive. I cover my ears as I prepare for the inevitable shock wave when...

"Uh, sir?" the soldier says. "My lighter's not working."

I walk over to the cell door and with a flick of my wrist the explosives are lit.

"Fire in the hole!" Jim shouts.

You don't need to tell me twice. I find a spot in a corner, then duck and cover.

The explosion is louder than I expected, and immediately sends me into a mini-panic attack. Was that too much? Too powerful? Turns out I don't have to worry; the charge is just right. Dad rushes out of his cell and grabs me like nothing else matters.

"I missed you so much," he says.

I tighten my grip around his waist. I'm never letting him go again. Never. I can't believe it. Against all odds, I got him back! I did it, me, a super-villain-in-training, and I managed to pull off the hardest test of all. I took over Dad's empire and I actually got him back alive.

All my repressed feelings and bottled emotions rush out in a big jumbled mess. I want to laugh and cry, sing and throw up, do cartwheels around the room and collapse into a corner and sleep for the next century. Instead, I hug my dad and let my happy tears soak his jumpsuit.

"So, I guess you like your present after all?" he asks.

I nod, laughing through the tears. "I love it, Dad. Best birthday present ever."

"I knew you could do it, Fiona." I look up at Dad. There's something in his eyes…something sparkling and alive. Pride. "I knew you could be the scorpion."

"Guys," one of the Storm Troopers speaks up, gesturing to Egghead, still standing there in his white lab coat with a gun jammed into his back. "What should we do with him?"

Jim looks at me, eyebrow cocked. "Your call, Fiona."

I know exactly what he's getting at. There's one thing and one thing only that an evil super-villain is supposed to do in this situation. I'm supposed to kill him, right? Now that he's no use to me, of course I'm supposed to kill him. But I'm not quite there yet. I'm not quite that evil.

"Stick him in there," I say, pointing to Dad's old cell. After one of the Storm Troopers shoves him in, I grab a pair of handcuffs and cuff him to the cell.

Egghead protests, but he knows he's lucky to be alive. After all, he's an unarmed scientist working in an evil lair. If he manages to survive to retirement, it would be the first time that ever happened.

Satisfied, Dad turns and heads for the door. Jim and the rest of the Storm Troopers follow. Dad is back in charge now, and not a moment too soon. "Major, we need to get the NOVA back."

Jim nods. "I couldn't agree more. Do you know where it is?"

"I overheard them talking about it. They keep it at the command center. So that's where we're going."

"Any idea what kind of opposition we can expect?"

Dad shakes his head. "I'm not going to lie, Major. There's going to be a lot of them. That's where The Captain is, so he's not going to leave himself unprotected. This is going to be a very tough fight."

"Just the way we like it," Jim grins, exchanging a fist bump with one of his men.

"Good man. That's the spirit." Dad smiles back. "And besides, it could be worse. At least they can't actually set off the bomb."

"Actually," I pipe up from the rear. "They can."

Dad stops, and then spins on his heel to face me. "What?"

"Jai…kind of has all three keys."

"Oh." Dad blinks. "Crap."

"Well put, sir," Jim gives him a cheerful pat on the back. "Now let's go get that nuke back. Squad, move out."

The trip up to the bridge is uneventful. The halls are surprisingly quiet. Maybe they're too scared of us and made a run for it, but I have a feeling that something's horrifically wrong.

"There." Dad points to a door up ahead. We sidle up to it, rifles trained and ready.

"Check the door," Jim whispers. A Storm Trooper jiggles the handle and flashes thumbs-up. It's unlocked.

"Okay, guys. On three." Once again, Jim holds up a gloved hand, and the Troopers tense, preparing to storm the bridge. "One…two…"

"Wait!" I whisper hoarsely.

Everyone freezes, except Jim. He just turns, giving me a questioning look.

"Blow the door."

He looks confused. "Why? It's not locked."

"This is an ambush, Jim." I'm guessing, but the more I talk, the more I'm convinced I'm right. "It's too quiet out here. It's too quiet because they're all in there, waiting for us. Blow the door."

Jim mulls it over, and then nods. There's a twinkle in his eye. I think he's actually impressed, but I'm not sure. It's hard to tell with him. "You heard the lady. Blow the door."

A Trooper wires the door with enough explosives to make me worry he'll snap the ship in two. I light the fuse, and we all take cover. Dad wraps his arms around me while I cover my ears, but nothing can prepare me for what happens next.

The explosion is so loud my eardrums nearly shatter. The shock wave knocks Dad and me to the ground, and the blast turns the metal door into white-hot shrapnel. Jim's the first one in, followed by the rest of his team. Without even thinking, I'm on my feet and charging in with him.

Turns out I'm right. The room is full of men, dazed from the blast. Even though they were expecting us, the explosion completely took them by surprise.

It doesn't take long before bullets whiz in all directions and lead fills the air. Everyone dives for cover, except me. Instead, I spot a group of The Captain's men hiding behind a control panel and send a fireball at them. The explosion shatters the wall-to-ceiling glass lining one side of the room, but I don't have time to admire my handiwork. Winding up, I get ready to throw another one when someone grabs me from behind, spins me around, and slams me up against a wall.

It's Jai.

All the fighting and gunfire seems to melt away. Time stops as I stare into the weird blue eyes of my former friend.

Then a long-overdue wave of anger hits.

So I headbutt him in his stupid face.

He stumbles backward with a startled yelp. Seizing the chance, I try to charbroil his face, but at the last second he grabs my arm, sending a ten-foot flame into a nearby wall. I'm on top of him now, the fire in my wrist matched only by the fire in my eyes. The only things that exist in the entire world are Jai, his butt, and the boot I'm about to lodge inside it.

My flamethrower growls, begging to be let loose.

"How would you like your face, Jai?" I spit at him. "Rare or well-done?"

"Good guys don't light people's faces on fire," he spits back.

"Maybe I can be the bad guy for once." I point my metallic arm at his backstabbing face.

"Stop!" A booming voice fills what's left of the bridge, halting us all in our tracks. "Drop your weapons or everyone dies!"

We all look to an elevated platform at the back of the room. A man in uniform is glaring at us. His face is so angular and bony he looks like a skeleton, wrapped with Saran wrap, trying to pass for a human. His lips are thin, cruel even, and his eyes are somehow even more intense than Jai's. He's wearing a captain's hat. In front of him is the NOVA.

My old coffee table looks just as I remember it—big, black, and heavy. Except for a panel I didn't know existed, which is open, exposing a row of lights. Two of the three are lit up.

Three lights. One for each key.

Wrapping his skeletal fingers around a familiar-looking silver chain, he inserts Jade's key into a hole in the panel. The last light blinks.

"Drop your weapons," he repeats, his tone cold and calculating.

The Storm Troopers look at each other. The blue men look at each other. I look down at Jai, and even he looks scared.

He's not actually going to do it, is he? Blow up his own ship? He can't possibly be that crazy.

Everyone freezes, their guns still pointing at each other. Nobody knows what to do. There's no training for this. No manual with step-by-step instructions. We eye each other, daring one another to blink. The Captain stands, his gaze unwavering, his sharp blue eyes waiting. If anyone's winning this staring contest, it's him.

With a clang, a metal door at the other end of the bridge opens, and Jade steps in, wielding a golden pistol. Ruby's close behind. They stand for a beat, obviously confused at the frozen chaos, and then they spot The Captain holding that key. What little color there is drains from their faces, making their terrified scarlet eyes look brighter than normal.

"Drop your weapons," The Captain says, holding our lives in his skeletal hand. "Now."

The silence is hot, heavy, and choking. Everybody's afraid to blink. It's so still you could hear a shell casing drop.

Dad breaks the silence.

"So this is how it ends?" he says dryly. "You know, I can't remember the last time all three of us were in the same room together." He chuckles. "Just like old times, huh?"

The Captain looks at him, then at Jade. "Yes," he says, nodding without a trace of emotion in his voice. "Just like old times."

And then he turns the key.

I squeeze my eyes shut and curl into a ball, bracing myself for the inevitable vaporizing blast. What will vaporizing feel like? Will I feel my skin melting or will I just turn into a pile of ash, like I had never existed?

I wait, holding my breath.

Except nothing happens.

Slowly, I crack one eye open, then the other.

The black stone top opens and the real NOVA comes out. The big black heavy thing I've been calling the NOVA this entire time isn't the NOVA at all. It's just the case.

It's metallic and round, like a steel basketball, rising slowly out of the black stone container. Some sections of it are made of something clear, like plastic or glass. As the NOVA continues its ominous ascent, the clear parts glow greener and brighter, and the entire thing hums. The sound is dangerous, dire.

The bomb is completely out of the case now, and across the front of the device, a panel of red numbers lights up and blinks, 5:00.

Five minutes.

"Ruby," Jade calls out, gold-plated gun still trained on The Captain. "Run. Get back to the chopper."

"But Mom! What about you?"

"Don't ask questions!" she shouts, her voice clogged with panic. "Just go!"

"There's no point," The Captain says dryly. "We both know the NOVA's blast radius is big enough to cover this entire island. If I set this thing off, it doesn't matter how fast you try to run. You won't make it."

Jade holsters her gun and puts up her hands as if she's trying to ward off a charging rhinoceros. "Listen, John, let's not do anything crazy here."

I blink. John?

"I know we've had our problems—"

"Problems?" he spits back. "After everything you did to me, is that what you call it? Problems?"

Jade glares at him. "That was fifteen years ago! Will you just let it go?"

Ruby jumps in. "Mom, what is he talking about?"

Jade turns to Ruby, her face burning as red as her eyes, almost...radioactive. "The thing is... Ah... You see... John and I...we were...kind of...in love."

"Don't forget the part where you cheated on me with Hawk," The Captain adds.

"Mom!" Ruby takes a step back, looking like she's about to throw up. "Eww!"

"Look," Jade says, getting redder by the second. I expect her head to explode in a shower of chunky red and white momentarily. "It was a long time ago, I was young and stupid, and John didn't look so...gross back then."

"**I AM STANDING RIGHT HERE!**" The Captain bellows.

Watching this preposterous exchange, my brain has trouble comprehending what I'm hearing. These are our parents, the ones we kids look up to, the ones who can do no wrong, the ones who always know the right thing to do. And yet, what I'm hearing, it sounds so...familiar. The rivalry, the petty bickering, the backstabbing, and the betrayal.

They're just like us kids.

Dad steps forward, like he senses the situation is spinning out of control. "Jade, maybe you should let me handle this."

"Let you handle this?" The Captain turns to face him. "And how do you propose to handle this, exactly?"

Dad straightens up, folding his hands behind his back. "Simple. We will take the NOVA back with us," he declares.

I wince, as does the rest of the room. Dad has never been a terribly good poker player.

The Captain's reaction is exactly what I expect. He laughs, once, twice, and then doubles over, howling. Somehow, even when he laughs, he sounds cold. "Do you honestly think I'm going to let you walk out of here with this bomb? Are you insane? After you stole it from us fifteen years ago, you think I'm going to let you take it again?"

Dad bristles. "I didn't steal it. I was keeping it safe."

"Safe?" The Captain shoots back. "Safe from what?"

"From you two!" The room is dead silent as Dad shifts his gaze from Jade to The Captain, and back to Jade again. "You," he points at Jade, "wanted to sell it on the black market to the highest bidder, if I remember correctly. And you," he gestures at The Captain, "were going on and on about nuking Russia, nuking China, nuking the Pentagon. I was afraid, John. I was afraid you were going to do something crazy. I was afraid you were going to do—" He pauses, scanning the room of soldiers, guns still pointed at each other, all waiting to die. "Well, this, basically."

The Captain snorts. "Well, it's better than what you did with it."

"I kept us safe, John."

"No you didn't. You wasted it," he says. "We built this bomb together. We built a bomb more powerful than any other bomb that's ever existed, and you just sat on it for fifteen years and did nothing with it."

"You—" Dad looks rather red, but at the last minute he stops himself, taking a deep breath. "You just don't get it, do you? You never understood."

"Get what? What don't I get?"

"That the NOVA isn't just a bomb." Dad slams a fist into his palm. "The NOVA is a doomsday weapon. You're not supposed to set off a doomsday weapon."

"Now who's crazy?" The Captain scowls at him, his electric-blue eyes even more intense. I swear, if he could shoot laser beams out of those things, we'd all be melted puddles by now. "What good is a bomb if you never set it off?"

"The NOVA isn't the weapon, John. The NOVA was never the weapon." Dad pauses, letting the words sink in. "Fear is the weapon."

Jai and I exchange glances. Both of us know exactly what he's talking about.

Dad keeps going. "Why do you think the government never came after us all these years?"

"Well, I have a battleship—"

"They have a battleship!" Dad exclaims. "They have a Navy. They have hundreds of battleships. That's not the reason." He takes a step forward. "They stayed away because they knew we had the NOVA. They stayed away because they were scared of what we would do with it." He takes another step forward. "I kept us safe."

"Enough." The Captain slams a fist down onto the black rock case, causing every frayed nerve in the room to jump. "Enough lectures." He turns to Jade. "And enough lies. I'm the one with the NOVA. I'm the one in control here. We do what I want."

All eyes are riveted on The Captain. The silence is so heavy, it's like we're all a thousand feet underwater. The tension is so thick you'd need a chainsaw just to make a scratch.

It's Jade who breaks the silence. "So what do you want, John?"

"Put your weapons down and leave."

"And then what?" Dad asks.

"And then the NOVA will be mine. Just like I've always wanted."

Dad pauses, looking thoughtful. "Why?"

The Captain frowns at him. "More games, Manson? Are we playing twenty questions?"

"Do you have somewhere else you'd rather be?" Dad shoots back. "Because if you do, please, leave! Nothing would make me happier." He crosses his arms. "Otherwise, answer my question. Why?"

The Captain focuses his laser-like gaze on Dad. "Because then I'll have power."

Dad shrugs like the word "power" means nothing to him. "Why?"

"Why?" The Captain repeats. "Why do I want power?"

"Yeah. Why do you want power, John?"

"Because…" He pauses, to my surprise. Clearly, nobody's ever asked him this question before. "Then everyone will fear me."

Another shrug. "Everyone already fears you."

"Not like this. With the NOVA, the fear me like they fear Death."

"So what? Why do you want that?"

The Captain pounds on the black rock again. "Because nobody messes with Death."

Dad blinks, looking stunned. "Is that it? Is that the real reason?"

"Yes. It is."

Dad turns to Jade. I have no idea what he's doing or where he's going with this. But if it keeps us all un-vaporized, even for another few minutes, I'm all for it. "Is that why you wanted to sell off the NOVA, Jade? So that you'd have enough money that nobody would come after you?"

Jade cocks her head thoughtfully, then nods. "Pretty much."

"My God," Dad smacks a palm onto this forehead. "My God."

Now I'm confused. The Captain's confused. The entire room is confused.

"Do you know what this means?" Dad continues.

Everyone in the room exchanges glances. None of us has a single clue.

Then Dad drops a bomb on us. Figuratively, of course. "We have been fighting each other for fifteen years, for literally no reason!"

The Kingpins look at each other. The super-villains look at each other. What is going on? What is Dad talking about?

"We aren't actually enemies." Dad gestures to all the soldiers in the room. "We all want the same thing. We all want our families to be safe. That's all that matters."

The Captain remains unmoved. "Yeah, and as long as I have the NOVA, my family will be safe."

"Safe?" Now it's Dad who spits words at him. I've never seen Dad like this. To me, Dad's always been this goofy person. Like a cartoon character. Someone who revels in the ridiculous. Someone who doesn't care whether he's taken seriously or not. But now? I'm taking him seriously. We're all taking him seriously. We hang on his every word. Our lives depend on it.

"Look at us." Dad gestures around the room. "Look what we've come to." He waves his hands in the air, as if trying to conjure up the words to describe how insane the entire situation is. "You're about to vaporize your own son! Is this safe, John? Is this what you want?"

Those icy eyes glare at Dad, unwavering. But then... something in those eyes seems to soften. Something seems to crack. Because even to seasoned soldiers, even to super-villains, this whole situation just feels...wrong.

Dad presses forward, sensing The Captain wavering. "We can keep our families safe, John. We all can. But only if we work together. Not like...this."

The wheels are turning, I can tell. The Captain's mind is working on overdrive, attacking his beliefs, challenging his assumptions. But still, his finger remains on the button.

It's a powder keg. That's the best way to describe it. We're all trapped in a powder keg, with no way out, with nowhere to hide. All it takes is one spark, one tiny spark, and we'll be turned into smoke and ash. The finger hovering over that button represents so much. So many people. So many lives. And right now, that finger is wavering. Like a rock on the edge of a cliff. Stay on or fall off? Stay on or fall off? It feels like the next thing anyone says will be enough to push it one way or the other.

The words that decide our collective fate comes from the last person I ever expected.

Jai.

"Dad, they're right." He steps out of his corner, shaking his head. "This is crazy. Even for us."

Jai's words seem to have an effect on The Captain, more than anything Jade or I or even Dad could've said. He shakes his head, taking a deep breath. "So what are you proposing, Manson? An alliance? Among the three of us?"

"Yes, an alliance." Dad nods. "The last time all three of us worked together, we produced this." He gestures at the glowing green NOVA. "Just think about what we could accomplish if we all worked together again."

The Captain stares at him, his face a stone mask. "Just like old times," he repeats, mulling the idea over, a smile slowly starting to creep in. It's a weird image, The Captain smiling. For a split second, I see something I never thought I'd see again. A ray of hope.

Finally, he says the word we've all been waiting for. "Okay."

Apparently, the entire room was holding its breath, because the moment that simple "okay" is uttered, the entire room lets out a sigh. Mortal enemies who had been shooting at each other shake hands, patting each other on the back. Even Jim cracks a smile. We're not all going to die after all. Not today.

The Captain peers at the control panel. "Which button disarms this thing?"

"Push the purple one," Dad says.

The purple one?

An alarm bell goes off in my head.

"Wait!" I scream. "Wait! Don't touch anything!"

But it's too late.

The Captain pushes the purple button. The actual purple button. And immediately, the bright-red five-minute timer blinks. And then it changes.

4:59.

The reaction of every person in the room is the same. Meaning, there is no reaction. No panic, no screaming, nothing. We stand in stunned silence as the red numbers count down. It's like we're all thinking, *No way. Those numbers can't actually be counting down. This can't actually be happening.*

We stand speechless until Dad starts the shouting match.

"You…idiot!" Dad screams. "What did you do?"

"I just did what you told me," The Captain shouts back.

Terror seeps out of my pores. This is real. This is happening. We're all actually going to die.

Dad marches up to the NOVA. "I said push the purple button. Purple!"

"I did!" The Captain jabs his finger at the control panel.

Dad stares incredulously. "That's the 'arm' button. The blue button. What's the matter with you?"

"That button is purple. Why would you tell me to hit the wrong button? What's the matter with you?" says The Captain.

Something inside me snaps. "Dad, shut up!"

They're supposed to be our parents, our super-villainous role models. Yet all they've done is act like children. And because of their idiocy, we're all going to be vaporized.

"Dad, why can't you just admit for once in your life that you're colorblind?"

"You're colorblind?" Both Jade and The Captain shout at once.

Dad crosses his arms. "I am not colorblind."

"If you're colorblind," The Captain spits at him, "then why did you make the buttons color-coded?"

"I'm. Not. Colorblind."

I groan, smacking a metallic palm into my forehead. Idiots. I'm going to die surrounded by idiots.

The timer continues counting down. 4:00.

I look at Jai. He's as pale as Ruby, who is shaking so hard it looks like she'll start bawling at any second.

The "grown-ups"—and I use that term in the loosest sense possible—continue bickering, oblivious to the fact that all our lives are in their incapable hands.

"Which button disarms it?" asks The Captain.

"You can't disarm the NOVA after it's been activated." Dad glares at him. "That wouldn't make a very good bomb, now would it?"

The Captain glares right back at Dad. "So what do we do now?"

"Let me think!" Dad strokes his goatee, and I can feel a tiny sapling of hope struggle into existence amongst the spiky radioactive rocks. He's thinking. It's not over yet. We might still get out of this.

Dad snaps his fingers. "Do you have any tools around here? Screwdrivers, wire cutters, that kind of thing?"

The Captain opens a drawer and fishes a bunch of tools out. "Here."

"Unscrew the access panel on the top—"

"It's your bomb! You do it!" he sputters.

"I can't," Dad says, holding up his cast. "Your thugs broke my arm, remember?"

Swearing, The Captain squints at the NOVA, screwdriver grasped in his shaking hand.

"Normally, you can't open it after the bomb's been armed because I built a secret tripwire in case any, you know, good guys try to disarm it. So you have to disable that first."

"Great. How do I do that?"

"Push the green button."

The Captain stares, bewildered. "What are you talking about?"

"The green button."

His eyes are wide, panicked. "Where— What do you—"

"What are you waiting for? Push the green button!"

"There is no green button!"

Oh. My. God. Captain Idiot and the Moron Patrol have led us all to the rocky cliff of nuclear doom, and they still can't get their act together to keep us from plummeting over it. If anyone out there is reading this, please make sure my tombstone says, *Here lies Fiona Ng. Killed by idiots.*

I shut off my flamethrower and storm up to them. "Give me that." I grab the screwdriver and shove The Captain aside with a metallic elbow.

3:00.

On the back of the NOVA is a control panel. It's full of buttons, oh-so-helpfully unlabeled except for a colored ring around each one. And on the top is the thin, almost-imperceptible outline of what looks like a square, removable plate. I flash back to my birthday, when we argued about this exact same thing.

Dad's green is a different color from the rest of the world's. He speaks his own color language, and I'm the only one who understands it.

My heartbeat drums in my ears, but I ignore it. My focus is laser-sharp. It has to be.

Let's see, when Dad says green, what he actually means is…

I push the yellow button.

The breath of every single person in the room seems to stop as the NOVA emits a high-pitched series of beeps, but the bomb doesn't go off. We're not dead. Yet.

I look up at Dad, and he nods back down at me. "That means the tripwire's disarmed. Go ahead."

I attack the screws as if my life depends on it, and it does. As I undo each screw, I can feel the full-on tsunami of freak-out building inside my chest. I fight it, hammering the waves back in my mind, but they keep coming. My hands grow shakier, my breathing more and more ragged, and droplets of sweat drip into my eyes, obscuring my vision.

Keep it together.

Finally, the sixth and final screw is out, and I look up at Dad. "You sure the tripwire's disabled?" I ask.

Dad nods, so I take a deep breath, and I open the panel. Or at least, I try to.

The metal is so smooth I can't get a grip on the edge of the access panel with my fingers. The panic starts to overtake me, but I swallow it back and push it down. Go away, Panic. I don't have time for you right now.

2:00, 1:59, 1:58...

"I need a knife." I call out. "Someone get me a knife."

Jade is beside me in a flash, holding out a gold-plated dagger. "Here."

It's long, sharp, and deadly-looking, with more jewels and sparkly things than a friggin' tiara. If this were any other time, I'd marvel at what a ridiculous, over-the-top waste of money this stupid thing is.

I take the knife and wedge the blade into the seam. I try to wiggle the blade back and forth, but it slips and slides over the metal, refusing to catch. I finally snag a corner and pry the panel cover off, but then my heart sinks as the cover clinks to the floor.

Holy. Crap.

A rat's nest of wires, cables, and electronic doodads stares back at me. It's completely indecipherable. How am I supposed to figure this thing out?

But Dad's one step ahead. He grabs a pencil and scribbles wildly on a piece of paper, like a scientist in the throes of madness. Something resembling a diagram takes shape on the paper, but it's all gibberish to me. Petrified, I glance at the timer.

1:00, 0:59, 0:58...

"I want you to find something that looks like a round silver disc, like a watch battery."

I peer into the rat's nest, harder than I've ever peered before. Watch battery. Watch battery. I move a jumble of wires out of the way with the blade of the knife, revealing the circuit board underneath. Something round and silver gleams back at me. "Got it."

"Now, find a red wire that's connected to it and cut it."

I look up at him. "You remember the colors of the wires from fifteen years ago?"

"I always use the same color scheme. It keeps me organized."

I look back at the rat's nest. Yeah. Organized. That's the word I would've used to describe this too.

The Captain shakily hands me a pair of wire cutters, and I peer into the maze of copper, searching for our salvation. Let's see, red wire, red wire. I don't see anything red.

Wait.

He doesn't mean red, does he? He means... He means...

For a brief, terrifying second my mind draws a blank. But then that life-saving color pops into my head, apologizing profusely for being so late.

I cut the brown wire.

"Okay, it's cut. Now what?"

"Now you need to find and cut a yellow wire connecting these." He points to his indecipherable diagram. "Brown box and purple cylinder."

Oh God. Too many colors. Let's see... Let's see... Yellow is green, brown is...red, and purple is...is...crap. What the heck is purple?

Blue. Purple is blue.

My mind races and sweat drips down my back, but I find the wire and I cut it. I glance at the timer. 0:32.

"Last one. There should be one long, white wire in there. Cut that one, and we should be done..."

White... White...

But this time my mind really does draw a blank.

What color is white? What color is white? Why can't I remember?

Wait. Isn't...isn't white the one color that actually means white?

I grip the single, long white wire. Behind me everyone sucks in a breath.

"Um…are you sure that's the right one?" Jade says.

I nod. White. White is white. Definitely…I think.

I look around. Jai's backed into a far corner, eyes wide, shaking uncontrollably. Ruby has her arms wrapped around her mom's waist, hugging her in a desperate death-grip. Twin black rivers of mascara run down her pale white skin. Huh. That's a first. I don't think I've ever seen Ruby cry before. 0:13.

Here we go. It's now or never. I'd better be right, or we're all toast. White wire, don't fail me now. I press the handles of the tool together and feel a twinge as it cuts through the wire.

Time stands still. All eyes are locked on the countdown timer.

Blink. 0:09.

Blink. 0:08.

Blink. 0:07.

No. I take a step back, shaking my head in disbelief. No, I don't believe it. It's still going. Why is it still going?

This can't be it. Not after everything we've been through. Not after how hard we all fought. How can this be how it all ends? White is white!

I look up at Dad, one last time, but he's not paying attention to me. Instead, he's frantically gesturing at the timer. "Look! Look!"

Blink. 0:06.

Blink. 0:06

Blink. 0:06.

18

There is no reaction. At first, anyway.

We all stand transfixed, staring at the flashing numbers, waiting to go over the nuclear cliff. We teeter ever-so-precariously above the precipice of doom.

The numbers flash 0:06 repeatedly. It's stopped counting down.

I'm the first one to make any noise. "YEAH!" I punch my metal fist in the air, and a wave of euphoria washes over the room.

Big, barrel-chested soldiers strong enough to lift cars hug each other and cry with relief. Others look ready to do cartwheels off the ceiling. Jai guffaws like a giddy blue-eyed hyena. And Ruby collapses into Jade's arms, her body shaking from the adrenaline. Even The Captain cracks an awkward, yellow-toothed smile.

And me? I'm doing my happy, I'm-not-going-to-die-today-and-I-just-saved-everyone's-collective-butts dance. It's a complicated dance, involving a lot of jumping around, hooting and hollering, and heedless flailing of the extremities.

However, then I swing my metallic arm a little too wildly, and I accidentally smack my wrist into the NOVA.

CLANG!

The clash of the big, bad nuclear bomb hitting the deck echoes as it rolls across the decking. It keeps rolling, and rolling, until it goes down a nearby flight of metal stairs.

CLANG!
CLANG!
CLANG!

The NOVA collides with every single step on the way down, and keeps rolling, before finally stopping against a control panel with a heavy-sounding **THUNK**.

We freeze in horror, eyes wide, hearts stopped—a room full of statues stuck in various states of celebration.

"Umm," I squeak, hands balled against my cheeks. "Why don't...we...go ahead and put that back in the case?"

I scamper over to where the bomb came to rest and carefully scoop it up, cradling it like a fifty-pound, nuclear-powered baby. A hundred pairs of horrified eyes follow me as I tiptoe my way back up to the NOVA container. And then, after placing it back into its receptacle, I twist the silver key that's still stuck in the control panel. Slowly, the disarmed and now slightly dented NOVA recedes into its case until the heavy stone top seals it into place.

And that's the story of how I had five heart attacks in one day

I suck in the fresh sea air in deep, grateful breaths the second we step outside. Sunlight. Blue sky. White clouds. I missed you all so! I never thought I'd see any of you ever again. Well, maybe clouds, but only of the giant mushroom variety.

Storm Troopers and blue-uniformed men, once mortal enemies, now walk side by side. Smiles fill their faces, and a few soldiers throw their heads back and laugh. Everyone seems as happy as I am to get out of the stupid control room.

Well, almost everyone.

"My missile launchers!" The Captain screams, surveying the smoking wreckage that had been his home. Clearly, his warm fuzzy feelings have evaporated, replaced by bitter grumpiness. At least now he doesn't have a nuclear bomb to take it out on. "Look what you did to my missile launchers!"

Dad dismisses his grumblings with a wave. "As far as I'm concerned, Jade did you a favor. What were they, Cold War era? I can have new launchers installed in two weeks that make those things look like pea shooters."

"Hmmm... New launchers..." The Captain scratches his salt-and-pepper stubble.

"So were you serious back there? About the three of us forming an alliance?" Jade asks as a group of her helicopters buzzes past.

"Of course I was serious." Dad's getting excited now, I can tell. "Think about how powerful we'll be. We'll have your air force, his naval force, and my Storm Troopers at our disposal. Not to mention my high-tech weapons labs, and a nuclear bomb to boot. Who could stand in our way?"

Now it's Jade that's mulling over the idea. "Interesting."

"I don't know why we didn't think of it before," Dad continues, arms gesturing wildly. "Most developed countries don't even have the kind of resources we'll have. Think about the evil schemes we could pull off together."

Jade's eyes light up. "We could rob Fort Knox. And steal the gold reserves."

"We could kidnap the UN," The Captain chimes in, starting to pick up on the excitement around him. "Those guys cut me off in traffic once."

Dad snaps his fingers, ignoring The Captain's insanity and gleefully replacing it with his own. "We could finally steal the Statue of Liberty. Just like I've always wanted."

Jade and The Captain both stop, turning toward him. "That's the stupidest idea I've ever heard," The Captain says.

Jade nods in a rare moment of agreement. "What would you possibly do with the Statue of Liberty?"

"What would I do? What wouldn't I do?" Dad beams but then, detecting a decided lack of enthusiasm for his idea, switches gears to petulant whining. "Come on. It's such a super-villain thing to do!"

Jade rolls her eyes. "Manson, why do you always have to be so melodramatic?"

"Melodramatic?" Dad says. "Me?"

I notice Jai standing in the distance, staring off into the sunset. I leave the "grown-ups" to argue and walk toward him. Ruby follows me.

"Hey," I say.

Jai turns. "Hey yourself."

"Crazy day, huh?"

He chuckles. "That's one way to put it." He nods at Ruby. "Whoa. You look really scary right now."

"Huh? What?" Ruby rubs her face self-consciously and looks down at her hands, now blackened with mascara. "Oh." Now that Jai mentions it, she actually does look kind of scary. Like a crazed, albino raccoon or something. "Shut up. Don't look at me." Ruby turns away.

Jai laughs. "It's fine, Ruby. Don't worry about it. Considering what almost happened, we're all lucky to look like anything right now."

Over in the distance, a swell of laughter rises up as our parents cackle at whatever plot they're currently hatching. I don't want to say definitively that it's evil laughter, over an evil plot, but few good ideas are accompanied by cackling.

Ruby turns back toward us. "So, does this mean we're all, like, best friends now or something?"

I snort. "I wouldn't go that far."

"Can we at least agree to stop trying to kill each other?" She crosses her arms. "After today, I don't think I want to see another explosion for at least—" She pauses. "At least a month."

Jai and I and the whole world know that there is no possible way that Ruby can go that long without blowing something up, but I don't call her out on it. Instead, I nod. "Sounds good to me. What about you, Jai?"

Jai thinks about it for a second, and then nods as well. "I'm down."

The three of us shake on it. Not best friends, but not mortal enemies. I think we can all live with that.

"Well then," Ruby coughs. "I think I need to wash some of this mascara off. Jai, where's the nearest bathroom?"

"Oh." Jai gestures toward the superstructure. "Just go in that—" He pauses, surveying the damage. "Well, that was a door, but go through that smoking hole you guys made. First room on your left."

Ruby nods and then heads off. But before she goes, she turns to me one last time. "Hey."

"Yeah?"

"You did good in there, Fireball."

I smile. Fireball. I could get used to that. "Thanks, Ruby."

Ruby leaves, and then it's just Jai and I, watching the sunset together. It's strange. I never realized how beautiful sunsets are. The way the sky lights up in a fiery blaze at the exact moment the sun kisses the water. It's like a symphony of light and color. I've been on this planet for thirteen years and I've never seen a sunset this beautiful before. I guess nearly being vaporized makes you appreciate stuff like this.

"It's...pretty, isn't it?" Jai says, avoiding my eyes.

"Yeah..."

The silence hangs between us, heavy, like a lead fog. The easy banter from before doesn't flow anymore. The words stick in my throat, refusing to come out. After all the betrayals and backstabbing, it feels like we're two different people. Like if we ran into old Jai and Fiona on the street, we wouldn't even recognize them. We'd look at them and think, dumb middle-school kids. Don't they know that life gets so much more complicated?

I miss Jai. The old Jai, I mean. The one I could just hang with. But old Jai and old Fiona are gone now. All we have left are these beaten, battered shells that have gone through something no kid should ever have to face.

Can things ever go back to the way they were? Do I even want them to? But then Jai, that big idiot, goes ahead and makes up my mind for me.

"I guess you were wrong, Sparky." He grins obnoxiously at me. "The bad guy didn't die at the end after all."

"I'm not your Sparky anymore." I look daggers at him. "My name is Fireball."

And then I haul back my metallic arm and shove him overboard.

He screams as he tumbles over the side and into the water. His flailing arms generate a mighty splash as he plunges into the blue.

And watching him fall, I learn the most important lesson about being an evil super-villain.

Sometimes, you can't help it. Sometimes, you just have to cackle maniacally.

Acknowledgements:

First of all, a huge thanks to our readers. Congratulations! Hopefully, you've enjoyed reading it as much as we've enjoyed writing it.

Next, to our agent-extraordinaire, Jamie Bodnar Drowley, who took a chance and believed in our weirdness, thank you for giving this story life. We're so proud to be riding the Jamie rocket ship to glory!

To our critique partners Amanda Foody, Stacy Stokes, Lindsey Prague, Roselle Kaes, Karma Brown, Abby Cavenaugh, and Paul Adams, thank you for being on Team LME and for helping us make this story the best it could be. You are all super talented, and we couldn't have made it this far without you.

To Jessa Russo, whose honest feedback sharpened our skills and made us better writers, thank you for taking the time to write back to us. Your heartfelt personalized note on our copy of *Ever* inspired us to never give up.

To Joanne Levy, who gave us invaluable advice about the publishing industry, thank you for being our mentor and showing us the ropes.

To our editor, Jennifer Carson, whose whip-smart edits made *Little Miss Evil* a much better story, thank you for supporting us every step of the way. Without you, we'd never be allowed to terrorize the public with our insanity. You are the awesome-sauce to our messed-up pasta.

To the Spencer Hill team, thank you for all your hard work and for making our dreams a reality. To my favorite teacher of all time, Mrs. Victoria Nutting, thank you for unlocking my passion and teaching me the power of words.

And finally, thanks to Japan for teaching us how terrifying little girls in school uniforms can be.

Sometimes
a lucky ritual
becomes a curse.

Seventh-grader Martin Cruz hates his rotten new town, Lower
Brynwood, but with his mom fighting a war in Afghanistan,
he has no other choice but to live with his crazy aunt. Then he
gets a message from a tree telling him it's cursed—and so is he.

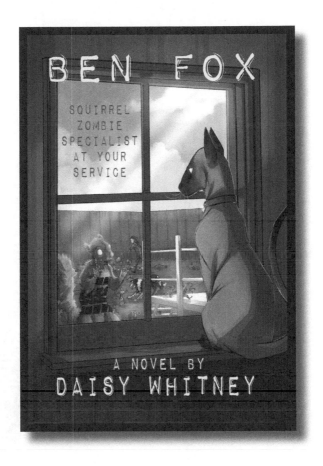

Ten-year-old Ben Fox has good friends, a great dog, and a lightning-fast little sister who drives him a bit batty. The only thing in the fifth grader's life that's truly annoying–well, besides having to wear braces on his feet every day–is the family's wily Siamese cat, Percy. Ben has always suspected something was off about Percy, who has never shown him or his beloved dog, Captain Sparkles, much affection.

But now he's sure something is off—Percy has raised an army of squirrel zombies in the backyard and they're ready to take on the dog.

About the Authors

Bryce and Kristy are a tag-team writing duo with way too many voices in their heads. As engineers living in Toronto, they can't be safely contained by mere cubicle walls, and therefore must spend every other waking moment writing to keep the crazy from leaking out at the office. When not writing or working, they spend their time parachuting into volcanoes and riding polar bears while tossing dynamite at rabid kangaroos. Yup, that's right. Sometimes they can't even believe how awesome their lives are.